Quality Maid

Mira Stables

For my sons, who wanted a really black villain.

Table of Contents

Chapter One

"DO hurry up, Clee, and tell us what he has to say," begged Faith. Clemency nodded absently, brows still knit over the lawyer's closely-written missive. The sisters were lingering over the breakfast table, though there was little in the meagre repast to stir the pleasures of appetite. Clemency abandoned the search for any note of hope in the letter and handed it over to her twin, Prudence, shaking her head despondently at Faith's expression of wistful hope.

"Nothing good, I'm afraid," she said. "So far as I can make out the mines are not producing anything. Mr. Morrison says there is no prospect of income from that source, and expresses the hope that the farm is prospering. I wonder how he thinks we have lived this past year! If it had not been for selling off the stock and letting the land, we must have starved. There was no money for labourers' wages. Perhaps he expected the three of us to turn farmer."

Prudence put the letter aside. "Town bred men have no understanding of country matters," she excused the absent lawyer. "I expect he thinks a farm runs itself. I'm sure we've done all that girls could in tending the poultry and the fruit and vegetable gardens. But if there is no money to come from those mines, what do we do now? I vow I'm ashamed to be seen in the village in this shabby old gown, and Faith's pink is positively indecent."

"I only wear it in the house," protested the youngest Miss Longden, putting her hands protectively across a sweetly rounded bosom which was certainly rather too clearly defined by the skimpy pink dress. "It's three years old and I've grown a lot since then. May *I* read the letter, Clee?"

Clemency handed it over. "Being shabby is bad enough," she said gloomily, "but we shall soon be cold as well. There was quite a sharp frost last night and the coals are nearly all gone and no hope of paying for more."

"Isn't there anything else we could sell?" asked Prudence; and then, tentatively, "Some of Mama's jewellery?"

"Papa would be sure to miss it," said Clemency. "He still spends hours in her room fingering her possessions and is quite convinced that some day she will come home. But I think he might let us use some of her dresses. I could say that after all this time they are quite out of fashion and that she would want everything new."

"And fine figures of fun we shall look in Mama's elaborate silks and velvets," groaned Prudence.

"They can be altered to more suitable styles, and at least they would cover us decently," said her twin, with a firmness developed over the years in which she had played mother to the other two, "and it was you who said that Faith's lustring was indecent."

Prudence subsided meekly. Faith looked up from the lawyer's letter. "You wouldn't think these mines could be just a take-in, would you? The names are so very respectable — El Christo de Lagas and Santa Brigida! I expect it was the names that induced Papa to choose them, though he really ought to know by now that names are nothing to go by. I mean — well — look at ours!"

"He thought they would bring him a fortune," said Clemency sadly. "And so did Mr. Morrison. Everyone who could afford to do so was buying South American mining shares. Papa can scarcely be blamed, especially as it was all for us. You know how little *he* cares for money. If it could bring Mama home or buy back his sight, it might be different. As it is, with Mama's money so oddly tied up, he thought to provide more comfortably for us. He still blames himself that Pru and I were never properly launched into Society, and already he is worrying about your come-out, Faith."

Faith chuckled. "The only thing I'm likely to come out of is this dress. Do you really think you can persuade him to let us use Mama's things, Clee? I hate to be a bother, but to speak truth my petticoat is in rags, and as for my stockings —" She lifted her shabby skirts to reveal much darned stockings of coarse white cotton.

"I'll ask him this very morning," promised Clemency.

"Which is all very well, and as you say, it may at least serve to cover us decently. But it won't pay for coals," objected Prudence. "I still think we ought to seek some kind of employment. Even if we did not earn much, we should at least have enough to eat, and Papa would be spared the cost of our keep."

"One of us would have to stay at home," Clemency pointed out. "Papa has learned to live with his blindness, but we could not all desert him."

"If only Mama would come back," sighed Faith, who was still young enough to hope for a miracle.

There was a sorrowful little pause. It was Faith herself who went on slowly, "Though it is hard to imagine what could have happened to her. Is it four years now, Clee?"

"Close on that," said Clemency briefly. It was not a subject that she wished to dwell on.

But Faith persisted. "Where could she have gone? And Elsie with her," she wondered for perhaps the thousandth time.

That was not the least part of the mystery. One grown woman might conceivably disappear in a busy town, but when Mrs. Longden had gone to stay with her godmother in Richmond in the county of Surrey, she had taken her maid with her, and it was during this visit that tragedy had struck. Mrs. Longden's health had given some cause for concern. The strain of nursing her adored husband through the grave illness that had followed upon a shooting accident, and the final shock of learning that his sight was irretrievably gone had told heavily upon her health and spirits. The family physician spoke anxiously of the possibility of decline. It was hoped that the change to a softer southern climate might prove beneficial, and she had been persuaded to pay a long promised visit to Mrs. Clare. Certainly her first letters after her arrival had seemed quite cheerful, and her spirits appeared to be reviving under the comforting influence of her godmother's gentle wisdom. But before the month was out she had grown restless and moody, fretting for home and blaming herself overmuch for her lack of fortitude in affliction. And then she had disappeared. Mrs. Clare, obliged to go out on business one morning, had returned to find both guest and maid vanished. No message had been left and all their belongings save Mrs. Longden's purse were still in the rooms she had allotted them. Thinking that they had perhaps gone shopping she had awaited their return throughout the afternoon. They had not come. Enquiries subsequently revealed that they had not been seen in Richmond itself, nor had they boarded any vehicle leaving the town. It could only be assumed that some passing traveller had given them a lift. But in spite of repeated advertisements and offers of reward, no such person had come forward. It was as though the earth itself had opened and swallowed them.

Over the years the twins had gradually come to accept the idea that they would not see their mother again, but their father remained confident that some day she would come home, and Faith, true to her name, shared his belief. Eighteen-year-old Clemency had taken over the reins of household management, and Prudence, whose talents were not domestic, had divided her time between her father and the outdoor activities of farm and garden. She read the papers to the blind man, played chess with him, patiently at first, guiding his fumbling fingers, and then with increasing zest as his powers developed until he was first her match and then, quite frequently, her master.

When days were sunny she walked abroad with him, describing the passing scene and warning him of approaching acquaintances so that he might be ready with a greeting, or perhaps he would sit with her as she worked in the garden, advising her as to the best situation for the plants that she was handling.

Apart from the continual aching anxiety over their mother's fate, life settled down into a comfortable if monotonous fashion, and if the twins had an occasional private moan over their vanished dreams of a London season they were young enough to feel hopeful of the hidden future and to take pleasure in the simple hospitalities of the neighbourhood. There was deep satisfaction, too, in their adored father's growing facility in overcoming his difficulties.

"At times one would scarcely know that he was blind at all," they assured one another proudly.

In the summer of 1824 Faith, now sixteen, came home from school and set about persuading her father that she was sufficiently educated for all practical purposes and need not return to that very select Harrogate seminary for young ladies. By way of proving her erudition she volunteered to take over the daily newspaper readings, thus freeing Prudence to help Clemency with the fruit picking and preserving that was now in full swing. And among the items that she read were glowing accounts of the vast profits to be made by investment in South American mining concerns.

To Faith, whose financial problems were limited to the hoarding of sufficient pocket money to buy birthday gifts for her family, the articles meant only a struggle with unfamiliar Spanish place names. To her father they sang a different song.

Of late he had been increasingly concerned over financial matters. His personal fortune was modest, but as his wife had been a considerable heiress the family had lived in comfort, even luxury, until her disappearance. It was then that the awkwardness deriving from the way in which her estate was tied up made itself felt. Felicity Longden's father had never wholly approved her marriage. While he liked John Longden well enough, he could not feel that a simple country gentleman was a worthy match for a girl who had received several far more distinguished offers. He perceived that his daughter had not inherited his own shrewd good sense if she could so permit sentiment to dictate her choice. Clearly she must be safeguarded against her weakness. It would be prudent to settle her fortune so that she should receive only its income during her life-time, the principal being tied up in trust for her offspring after her death. His prospective son-in-law was as careless as Felicity. Concerned only with the prospect of calling his beloved, 'wife' at the earliest possible moment, he raised no objection to this rather disparaging arrangement, an attitude which only confirmed Mr. Hasledon's poor opinion of his business capacities. That careful man had proceeded to arrange matters safely, as he thought, for the pair of simpletons. He could not be expected to foresee the tangle caused by his daughter's disappearance, and since he had died several years before that tragedy occurred he was not then in a position to set matters right.

Since Mr. Longden was resolute in refusing to presume his wife's death, his daughters could not inherit. This would not have mattered if they could have continued to draw on the income from the Hasledon estate, but this, too, was denied them, by an arrangement made in haste at the time of Mr. Longden's accident that his wife should have her own account with the bank. The fortune that had comfortably sufficed his bachelor needs was insufficient to support his family. The South American venture seemed to offer a heaven sent answer to all his difficulties. With all the enthusiasm of the tyro, he had plunged recklessly, hesitating only as to whether the Serena mine should make his fortune rather than the Santa Brigida, for as Faith had shrewdly guessed, the names of the mines had worked powerfully upon his fancy.

But the months passed and there was still no sign of the promised golden harvest. The girls had conspired to shield him from the full knowledge of the abject poverty to which they were reduced, hoping each day that the luck would turn. Mr. Morrison's letter had finally quenched that hope. The mining venture was a calamitous failure.

"We simply must *do* something," said Prudence determinedly. "The summer has been bad enough, but I can't and I won't face a Yorkshire winter on a diet of potatoes and cabbage with a precious egg for an occasional treat. You've no notion how hungry one gets working out of doors. I'm beginning to understand how starving people can bring themselves to steal food. I've nearly forgotten what roast beef tastes like, and I'm sure if I met an unattended sirloin I should promptly succumb to a life of crime."

It was laughingly, playfully said, but Clemency knew that the laughter masked the bitter truth. Pru really did suffer from hunger pangs. What was more, the work she did in garden and poultry yard was too much for a girl. Studying her twin with eyes grown anxiously perceptive, Clemency realised that she was much too thin. Perhaps it was her fading summer tan that made her look pale and sickly, but that did not account for the sharp angling of her jaw and the hollows at her neck. In strong contrast to her own slight fragility, Pru was tall, built on noble Junoesque lines. This morning in the sharp October sunlight she looked almost gaunt. Clemency's soft lips firmed to a resolute line.

"Very well, then," she said quietly. "What kind of work can we do?"

"I've always wanted to be an opera singer," volunteered Faith eagerly.

Clemency repressed a twinkle. "I fear Papa would never consent to such a scheme," she said, treating the absurd suggestion with proper deference. "Nor would it meet our present need, since a long and costly training would be needed before you could hope to tread the boards."

Faith protested unavailingly. She was sure that her untrained voice was adequate to chorus work and even to minor roles, while diligent study would soon raise her to the ranks of the prima donnas. She was only convinced that her scheme was quite ineligible, at least at present, when Pru pointed out that she could scarcely hope to make the right impression on a theatrical manager when she was so shabbily dressed.

There was a thoughtful silence. It was really very difficult. None of them was sufficiently highly educated to take a post as a governess, and what other position was sufficiently genteel to be acceptable to their father?

Into this silence came Betsy, to enquire if the chicken broth would suffice for their nuncheon, or should she put some potatoes to bake in the embers?

Pru groaned. "I think I shall seek a post as housemaid to a master butcher," she said hungrily. "At least I should get enough to eat!"

"Little enough you know about it, Miss Pru," said Betsy. "Lucky if you got bread and dripping. Folk in that class don't bother to treat servants properly. Nor they wouldn't employ anything as elegant as a housemaid.

Maid of all work, that's what you'd be, and a reg'lar little slavey, at everyone's beck and call the livelong day. You'd soon be thankful for a bowl of Betsy's good broth to stay your stomach." She began to clear away the breakfast dishes with an audible sniff that indicated her hurt feelings.

Pru put an arm round the bent grey-clad shoulders and hugged the old woman warmly. "Now, Betsy-love, you know I meant no disparagement to your cooking. We think you're wonderful, producing such savoury dishes out of next to nothing. But don't tell me you wouldn't be thankful to set eyes on a baron of beef. You must be just as tired of pinching and contriving as we are."

Betsy softened a little and admitted that it would be a real pleasure to deal faithfully with a decent joint again. "Had that lawyer gentleman any better news?" she demanded, for having brought in the letter and being wholly in the girls' confidence she was well aware of its importance.

Pru shook her head ruefully. "No hope at all. That's why we were talking about seeking situations. We're all young and strong and willing to work. Surely there must be something we could do?"

The girls were not the only ones who had been worrying about ways and means. Betsy cared little that she had received no wages for months, and though the girls had urged her to seek another situation where she might be comfortable and well paid, not for *twenty* golden guineas a year would she desert her former nurseling's children in their need. Cunningly she had dipped into her own savings to purchase small items whose provenance would never be suspected. Miss Clee never wondered why a pound of butter lasted so long, or how it was that they never seemed to lack spices and flavourings. But for all her care and skill the stores in the house were visibly dwindling, and even better than her three charges Betsy knew that something drastic must be done. She had already made her own plan of campaign and had only been awaiting a suitable moment for broaching it. One had to go cannily with Miss Clee. Plaguily proud she could be at any hint of seeking patronage or charity, and her more easy going sisters would certainly follow her lead. Now it seemed that her opportunity had come.

"It's not for the likes of me to be knowing what young ladies could do, but there's others could advise you well enough if some folk weren't too proud to seek help."

There was a glint in Clemency's eye. She and Betsy had differed on this head before. "If it's Lady Eleanor you're meaning, Betsy, it's no good. She's been far too kind to us already, and she's not a wealthy woman. If she knew the fix we are in, she'd just *invent* a post for one of us, and I simply will not hang on her sleeve to that extent."

Pru promptly seconded this view, exclaiming, "No, indeed. It's quite bad enough with Giles sending over fresh milk every day for never a penny payment and vowing it would only be poured away. Which it would not, for they would use it to fatten the piglets."

Faith giggled. "Does he think to fatten us?" she enquired. But Pru, who was not unaware of the masculine charm of Lady Eleanor's son, refused to be amused. It irked her sorely that even in so small a way they should be his pensioners.

The single minded Betsy ignored these irrelevant interruptions. Fairly launched at last upon her project she was not to be deflected. "Not Lady Eleanor," she told Clemency, "though I've no doubt she'd give her nephew the benefit of her advice. I'm thinking it's Captain Kennedy you should apply to. And no need to think you'd be under an obligation to *him*, for didn't your own father save his life, and him no more than a bairn? It's thankful the man would be to be put in the way of doing you a service."

Any one of the girls could have passed a strict examination on the story of how their father's swift action had saved the infant Piers Kennedy from a horrid death. The tale had been a great favourite in their nursery days, with its moment of spine chilling tension as the mad dog raced straight for the toddling babe and its dramatic climax as their father shot the brute in the nick of time. The tale had lost nothing in Betsy's telling and the little girls had listened spellbound. But that had all happened thirty years ago, and, to Clemency, the tenuous claim on Captain Kennedy's gratitude was not one that she cared to press. It was not as though they were even acquainted with him. A naval career had kept him from home for years and during the brief intervals of shore leave it had so chanced that they were either still in the nursery or away at school. It was fully six years since he had last been in Yorkshire, and they had fallen into the way of regarding his cousin Giles, who acted as his agent, as lord of the manor.

"There might be someone among his fine friends who stood in need of a governess or a companion," Betsy went on. "It's only a start you need — just to introduce you and maybe speak a word in your favour. His friends might well be glad to hear of such respectable young ladies."

Faith laughed. "Respectability is not our strong suit just at the moment. Prue has just been saying that I'm positively indecent. And maybe Clee could be a governess, since she's the only one of us who's the least bit bookish, but I'm sure I couldn't. I might be an abigail or a seamstress though. What do you think, Clee?"

"I don't see how a naval officer could usefully advise us on such feminine matters," declared Clemency roundly.

But Pru was inclined to side with Betsy, and since Faith was eager to do something, anything, rather than drag on in their present miserable fashion, Clemency found herself outnumbered. Reluctantly she agreed that Captain Kennedy should at least be approached.

Fierce argument then broke out over the choice of ambassadress. Faith, a willing volunteer for the task, was promptly snubbed by her elders as too young and irresponsible. Captain Kennedy could not be expected to treat a mere child seriously. Since Clemency was the elder by a full quarter of an hour, Pru thought that she should undertake the mission, while Clemency felt that Pru, whole-heartedly in favour of the scheme, would be a better advocate. Finally they agreed to draw lots for it, the loser to undertake the all important errand, and as might have been expected in face of her reluctance, Clemency was that loser.

"Just my luck!" she lamented. But when Pru relented and offered to go in her place, she refused, saying that they must abide by the luck of the draw or they could not expect the plan to prosper. Instead they had best marshal their combined resources to equip the envoy as respectably as possible for the interview on which so much depended, and with this laudable object in view the meeting adjourned to Clemency's bedchamber.

Chapter Two

"WON'T your honour consider taking the lad back in the stables?" asked lodge keeper.

Piers Kennedy shook his head in decided negative. "I'll not trust him with animals again, Grant. Because he's your nephew and for that reason alone, I've told my cousin he may employ him in the gardens. His thoughtlessness will do less harm there."

The voice, perfectly pleasant and friendly, yet held a note that put argument at a discount. Nevertheless Jim Grant determined on one more appeal. "He's not a bad lad, Sir," he urged. "His mother did her best to bring him up decent, but 'twas a losing battle against that smooth-tongued cheating rascal she married on. You couldn't expect the lad to be as steady and reliable as another. But there's good in him, Sir, I swear there is. He needs a firm hand, I'll allow. That's why I'm wishful to keep him here under my own eye rather than let him go off to strangers."

"You will be well able to keep an eye on him if he is working in the gardens."

Grant shuffled his feet uneasily and his eyes shifted away from the cool blue gaze that measured his honesty. "I doubt the gardens'd be too slow for him," he blurted out. "He's a lad that's used to getting about — reg'lar fly-by-night his dad was — always moving on whenever he'd made a place too hot to hold him. Gardening's too slow for a lad like young Will. Stables is different. Always a bit o' summat going on there. It's livelier like for a younker, and there's no denying he's a rare hand with the horses. That'll be the gypsy blood in him. Couldn't you give him another chance, Sir? I'm sure he's as sorry as could be about the colt. 'Twas only a lad's pride in the way he could gentle the beast when t'other lads could do nowt wi'it."

Piers Kennedy's black brows met in displeasure. He was unused to having his decisions disputed. "A little more than that I think, Grant," he said coldly. "A youngster's mischief I could forgive, even though it has ruined the work of years of careful breeding. But he's eighteen, old enough to know better; and to run off and leave the poor brute lying in agony after

16

his own reckless tricks had broken its legs, I cannot pardon. If he had found the courage to go to my cousin and own up to his misdeeds, Dark Star could have been put out of his misery. He thought of his own skin rather than the horse's suffering. I'll not employ him again in my stables. The offer of a job in the gardens is still open."

Grant shook his head slowly, accepting defeat. "Don't know as I blame you, Sir," he admitted with gruff honesty, "but a man has to do the best he can for his own. 'Tain't no manner of use me saying yes to your offer. Will 'ud never stand it. I'll have to think of some other ploy to keep him out of mischief."

And I devoutly hope you may succeed, thought Piers, as the heavy footsteps crunched away down the drive. A lad with Will Overing's doubtful antecedents was a problem. Piers fancied he knew the type. Brash, idle, glib liars, it was never their own failings that were to blame when Nemesis eventually caught up with them. In his younger, less cynical, days, Piers might have admitted Grant's plea for a second chance for the lad. That was before he had acquired his limp and the white lock that streaked his dark head, mementoes of a murderous attack by a convict whom he had tried to help during the years he had spent in Australia. The man had been just such a plausible rascal. The attack had wrecked Piers's naval career and only a magnificent constitution and grim determination had saved his life. He felt sorry for Grant, decent steady going fellow that he was, but he was not sorry that his offer had been rejected.

With a slight dismissive shrug he turned to more cheerful matters. It was still only mid morning, a crisp October day with a hint of frost and the tang of burning leaves hanging on the still air. He would take out a gun and see if eye and hand had lost their old cunning. There had been scant time for sport of late, but today he would give himself a holiday. He made briskly for the gun room, weighing the choice between Taviston moor which was convenient of access and Keylesden which meant some rough walking but would probably offer better sport.

In the event he was not destined to visit either on that particular October morning, for Beach stopped him just as his hand was outstretched to the gun room door. Beach had been his servant during his seafaring days, had tended him faithfully during that bad time six years ago, and had been installed, with his wife, at the Dower House when Piers had decided that it provided ample accommodation for a bachelor on his rare visits and had turned over the Manor House to his aunt and cousin.

"Lady asking to speak with you, Captain, Sir," announced Beach. "Miss Longden."

The name had a familiar ring, but Piers could not quite place the connection. "Alone?" he enquired with a trace of surprise.

"No, Sir. Got an abigail along o' her. I showed them into the morning room."

Piers sighed. "Very well," he conceded reluctantly. Females never knew how to come to the point. They wasted hours in tedious circumlocution before broaching the simplest matter. Doubtless by the time that this one had stated her errand it would be too late to take out a gun. "You can show her into the library in five minutes."

He was seated at the writing-table when the expected knock came, an impressive array of papers indicating that he was much occupied and had little time to waste on unknown importunate females. He was sure that he did not number anyone of the name of Longden among his intimate acquaintance. Probably some earnest creature was seeking subscriptions for some charity or other.

He rose politely as Beach announced the visitor, a little startled that instead of the austere and elderly female of his imaginings his caller was only a slip of a girl, and, having recovered from this initial shock, at some pains to swallow his involuntary grin at the wench's extraordinary appearance. He was no expert on feminine fashions, but no one could fail to notice the incongruity between her expensive if somewhat ornate dress, her scuffed and shabby shoes and a feather trimmed bonnet, slightly too large for her, which tilted rakishly to one side as she gravely curtsied her acknowledgement of his greetings. She looked just like a little girl dressed up in her mother's clothes. He could not, of course, know how accurately he had assessed the situation.

A wave of furious colour dyed the tightly composed little face as the girl straightened the absurd headgear. Piers, hitherto divided between irritation and amusement, noticed that her fingers were shaking visibly, and took pity on her.

"Miss Longden?" he enquired kindly. "Will you not be seated? I regret that I do not at once recall the occasion of our meeting. I must plead long absence as my excuse and beg you to refresh my memory and then to tell me how I may serve you."

His courtesy did not succeed in setting the girl at ease. She remained standing with downcast head, wrenching nervously at the string of her reticule which had somehow become twisted round her wrist, before she eventually found the courage to raise honest brown eyes to his face and say bluntly, "You have not forgotten, Sir. So far as I know you never *have* met me before. But I believe you to have been pretty well acquainted with my Papa, and it is upon that score that I have presumed to thrust myself upon your notice. For your other surmise is correct. I have indeed come to — to —" She stopped. Somehow, under the assessment of those cool blue eyes, she could not bring herself to utter the humble, "to beg your help" that she and Pru had agreed upon. Her chin went up as she hastily substituted, "to ask your advice." It was a grave tactical error. Piers would probably have responded to the open appeal of the first phrase. As it was he merely begged her once more to be seated, indicating a chair which faced the writing table. She poised herself on its edge with the anxious precision of a schoolgirl anticipating rebuke, shabby shoes set demurely side by side on the muted glow of the Persian rug.

Wishful to be done with the interruption to his day as speedily as good manners would permit, Piers did not pursue the question of his acquaintance with Papa, but said only, "I am naturally honoured by your choice of counsellor. Pray continue."

Intent on the best way of presenting her case without too far demeaning her family pride, Clemency missed the satirical note in his voice and plunged into her story.

"I must first explain, Sir, that Papa has recently suffered a reverse of fortune because of the failure of certain South American investments," she brought out baldly, and he felt a momentary touch of pity for the girl, young and gently bred, driven by expediency to such a distasteful task.

"My sisters and I," she went on, "wish to seek respectable situations of some kind, at least for two of us, since Papa cannot be left entirely alone in his affliction. We thought you might know of some family among your friends who could offer us employment. We are not especially skilled, I'm afraid, but we would work hard and we would not expect high salaries. Papa would thus be relieved of the burden of our support."

The stilted phrases came to an end and the speaker breathed a sigh of relief and fixed expectant eyes on Captain Kennedy's face. It did not look very encouraging. The dark brows were frowning, the mouth firmly set, almost grim. She could not know that her prim words had taken him half across the world. His friends! He thought of their primitive homes, of the women convicts that one or two of them employed. This foolish little chit had no idea of the conditions of living in that new world. But of course not. She probably supposed him to have a wide acquaintance in his own country, possibly even in London, which seemed to be the Mecca of all young females of marriageable age. He wondered how much of the desire for employment was genuine need and how much was simple boredom with quiet country living. And what, he speculated, was Papa's affliction, apart from the possession of daughters with oddly independent notions? His frown deepened.

"I would advise you to discuss your difficulties with my aunt," he said coldly. "I assume that you are acquainted with her. She would be better able to help you to a suitable establishment than any mere male."

Clemency coloured furiously. "Lady Eleanor has already been kindness itself," she said. "I will not impose further upon her good nature."

"May I ask if your father has any notion of your intentions, or indeed, of this visit?" he enquired.

The downcast eyes were answer enough.

"I thought not. Let me assure you, Miss Longden, that a man would rather suffer the direst poverty than cast his daughters upon the world. And if his circumstances do not permit all the extravagances of fashion," with a sardonic glance at her rich silk gown and expensive, if ill fitting, bonnet, "his children must accept this in good part. If you really wish to spare your father's purse, it would better become you to study the domestic arts and practise economy."

His tone was cold and critical. Clemency's heart sank. Clearly it had been a mistake to wear Mama's clothes. And how could she bring herself to tell this unsympathetic stranger that it was not a case of mismanagement and extravagance, but of actual hunger?

After all the effort the visit had cost and all the hopes that had been built on its success, she could see herself going home to admit failure. Bitter resentment overwhelmed the years of careful schooling, and she flared out at him. "I regret having wasted your time, Sir. I had believed, foolishly it would appear, that a gentleman never forgot an obligation, and so was misled into the belief that you would welcome the opportunity of serving my father's children. I acknowledge my mistake and will bid you good morning."

She rose with an energy that set the bonnet perilously a-tilt, accorded him an infinitesimal bow, and moved swiftly to the door.

"One moment, Miss Longden," snapped the voice behind her, and the rasp of command checked her impetuous haste in spite of herself. "What talk is this of obligation? I am aware of none. You will kindly explain your meaning."

He, too, had risen, and now he came round the writing-table towards her. She was dimly aware that he limped a little. Scarcely a limp, rather a slight inequality in his gait that she promptly forgot as she faced the anger in his blue eyes.

It was a little frightening, she acknowledged, but exciting too, and since the odious creature had obviously no intention of helping them there was no reason why she should allow herself to be browbeaten. She curled her lip at him.

"It is no part of my duty, Sir, to explain to you the code of behaviour customary among gentlemen. In any case," she elaborated with relish, "it would clearly take far too long, and my time is too valuable to be squandered so," and she curtsied again, defiantly, as her fingers closed on the door handle.

A powerful grip closed over hers. "You little spitfire!" said the deep voice, amused now, and very close to her ear. "Let go that handle at once and answer my question."

There was no option but to obey the first part of the order, since the iron grip on her wrist was forcing her to release her hold and swinging her round to face him. Clemency had never been so roughly handled in all her sheltered life. She had spent a very trying morning, and now, between pain in her maltreated wrist and fury at the man's calm assumption of authority, lost her temper completely. Her left hand flashed up to deliver a resounding slap across that smiling mouth.

The action was purely instinctive and repented even as it was made, but the damage was done. The dark head jerked upward at the blow, then the smile deepened as he stooped to catch the impetuous hand and hold her prisoner by both wrists.

"Now what do you think you deserve for that, Miss Longden?" he asked gently. "You would have done better you know, to stick to the use of your tongue, which seems to be perfectly adequate to the infliction of insults. But since you are so well versed in the code of behaviour appropriate to gentlemen, you will be aware that since *you* struck the blow, *I* am entitled to demand satisfaction. However, I will be generous to youthful folly and accept an apology."

Apology — sincere regret for a most unbecoming action — was actually trembling on the tip of her tongue, but at this provocative speech the soft lips folded together in resolute defiance.

"No?" enquired her tormentor, now definitely enjoying the situation. "Not even to have your hands released so that you may set your bonnet straight?"

Insult upon insult! The wretched bonnet had descended over one eye as she raised her hand to strike, and she knew only too well how ridiculous she must look. She subdued a strong impulse to kick, even bite: anything to crack that imperturbable, deeply amused façade. Dignity — so far as the bonnet would permit — was the only possible role. She assumed an air of calm detachment, allowing her wrists to lie limp and passive in his grasp, her eyes to gaze pensively at that intriguing plume of white that marred his dark head, and only her tight-pressed lips betrayed her seething fury.

"I am waiting, Miss Longden," reminded the inexorable voice. "Your apology, if you please, or I shall resort to stronger measures."

An empty threat, that. There was nothing he could do. No need as yet to submit meekly. She managed a sweet, if artificial, little smile.

"Indeed, Sir?" she said politely. "Then I trust you have no pressing engagements this morning, for you are like to have a long wait."

Privately Piers was inclined to admire her spirit, though he considered that she stood sadly in need of schooling. Papa had certainly neglected his paternal duties. The young minx would be all the better for a sound spanking, but he could scarcely take it upon himself to administer *that* form of correction. If he were not to lose face by tamely releasing her there was only one thing to be done, and he wasted no time on thinking of possible repercussions. A swift jerk on the captive wrists and she was in his arms, his kiss pressed ruthlessly on the soft young mouth. For a moment, taken utterly by surprise, she lay unresisting against his breast. Then realisation came and she strove with all her puny strength to break free of his hold, writhing and kicking out furiously.

Piers had meant only to teach the girl a sharp lesson on the unwisdom of intruding upon strange men with requests for help. That one kiss had been the limit of his intentions. But the feel of the soft little creature struggling so frantically in his arms aroused a primitive desire to conquer and subdue. Not for worlds would he really hurt her, but she should learn that he was master. He simply held her caged in the steely strength of his arms until she grew breathless and exhausted and her struggles ceased. Then he gathered her closer, holding her in the circle of one arm while his free hand loosed the ribbons of that unfortunate bonnet and tossed it aside. He kissed her again, a kiss that even the frightened untaught girl in his arms recognised as very different from that first swift punitive one. He kissed her firmly, demandingly, but there was nothing greedy or brutal about it. His mouth was warm and beseeching, and despite her rage and shock Clemency felt herself yielding to its beguilement. She was too weary to fight any more and not even sure that she wanted to, held in a dream that brought new and delightful sensations and innocently unaware of the desire that was leaping to life in the man who held her.

It seemed an age, a blissful age, before he raised his head and looked down at her, an odd expression in the blue eyes, an uncertainty, a questioning that was quite new to him. Clemency sighed a little, aware that the dream was over. She looked up into the hard masculine face so close to her own and shivered at the impact of its vigorous reality. No dream, but fierce, exciting, frightening fact.

Piers felt the shudder that shook the slight frame and took it for revulsion. At once he released her, only keeping one hand beneath her elbow for support as he guided her to a chair, for she was white and shaken now that reaction was setting in. He himself had undergone a shattering experience. He had teasingly demanded an apology from a pretty and foolishly behaved girl, but no apology could possibly cover his own subsequent conduct. He could not understand how the situation had suddenly snapped from the trivial and light hearted to the vitally important. He was no believer in pretty romances founded on love at first sight, and in any case, at first sight he had thought his visitor a plaguey nuisance. The quite different emotions which now filled his heart were much too new-born to be reliable. Conscious of a strong desire to gather the little creature into his arms and pet and soothe her back to confidence, he marched firmly to the fireplace and rang for Beach, leaving her to recover her composure as best she might.

Having desired the servant to bring coffee and cakes he picked up the ill-fated bonnet, absently smoothing and folding its crushed ribbons as he sought for words to bridge the embarrassed silence. The girl sat with drooping head, a pathetic little image, her childish pride humbled, her newly emergent womanhood bewildered and astray. Mercifully Beach was swift in returning with the coffee. Piers dismissed him with a nod of thanks and poured out the powerful brew which was made to suit *his* tastes before recalling that a girl might prefer a milder beverage. He added cream liberally in an attempt to mellow the bitter stuff and carried the cup to her side.

"Do you take sugar in your coffee?" he enquired politely, in such ludicrous contrast to his recent behaviour that even he perceived its oddity yet was too disturbed to smile.

Clemency saw the cup as something normal and homely in a world gone suddenly crazy. Her hands came out to take it as a man struggling in deep water clutches at any support. But the cup chattered on its saucer in her shaking fingers and she was quite incapable of answering his simple question. She managed somehow to lift the cup to her lips and sipped gingerly at the mess of cream floating on the surface. The potent scalding brew certainly revived her so that she was able to focus on her host standing attentively beside her with the sugar bowl in one hand and a plate of sponge fingers in the other. "Or would you rather try a macaroon?" he offered. "Mrs. Beach makes them and they are really very good."

Clemency had a vague notion that she ought to refuse to break bread — or in this case, sponge fingers — in the house of a man who had behaved so shockingly, but she was suddenly aware that she was exceedingly hungry. She had been too wrought up to eat breakfast and the long walk to the Dower House had tired her. Then had come that unreal interlude with this very strange man who was now treating her rather as though he were an anxious nurse tending a sick child. She had not tasted coffee for several poverty stricken months. It was ambrosial. It seemed that she was totally lacking in the sensibility proper to a delicately bred female. Her hand was stretching for a cake almost of its own volition.

Captain Kennedy heaved a sigh of relief and his grim countenance softened almost unbelievably as she stripped off her glove and bit into the sweet morsel, quite unaware of the creamy rim about her mouth that gave considerable substance to the nursery image. He left the cakes strategically to hand and retired to the table to pour his own coffee, taking his time about the business and noting in some surprise the inroads that his frail little adversary was making on the cake plate when she thought he was not watching.

Silently he saluted her courage. She was not going to treat him to a fit of the vapours, though heaven knew she had sufficient cause. He would let her drink her coffee in peace and then make some attempt to put their relationship on a better footing. It had become important that she should forgive him — not just at once perhaps — that was scarcely to be expected — but quite soon, if he worked hard on his apologies and promises of future good behaviour; which brought him up with a round turn, for there was nothing he desired so much as to kiss her again, and that ridiculous creamy rim on the adorably curved upper lip was a flagrant invitation. Hastily he averted his gaze and passed her the neglected macaroons.

He was hesitating between frank apology, casting himself entirely upon her mercy, and the more risky course of pleading irresistible temptation, when an interruption occurred that denied him the opportunity of doing either.

A pleasant baritone voice was uplifted in cheerful song outside the window, bidding dull care begone. It broke off abruptly to be succeeded by a peremptory tapping on the glass.

"My cousin, Giles. You will know him, of course. Shall I bid him begone with his song, or may I admit him?" said Piers in rapid explanation, inwardly cursing his cousin's inconvenient timing.

But Clemency obviously welcomed the interruption and said, in some surprise, "But of course you must admit him. Why not?"

Piers had not the heart to suggest that there was anything questionable about a young lady being found alone with a gentleman in that gentleman's residence, even if she had an abigail — whose presence he had forgotten until that moment — in attendance somewhere about the place. If the events of the past quarter of an hour had not taught her the danger of such behaviour he no longer had any desire to ram the lesson home.

The rapping on the window was repeated, embellished now by sundry hails which Giles fondly believed to be of a nautical nature. "Hey there, Captain! Ahoy! Open up! Permission to come on board?" And as Piers at last acceded to the repeated demands, "What are you doing skulking 'tween decks on as fine a morning as we're likely to get this month? I looked for you over Taviston as I came down. But what's all this?"

His eye lit upon that fatal bonnet, now reposing demurely on the gleaming oak of the writing-table. "Piers! You old devil! Who've you got hid —" His voice failed and died completely as he spied Clemency. For just one second he gaped visibly. Then as she smiled her greeting he made a swift recovery. "Clee! I scarce recognised you. Why the sartorial splendour? Surely not to call on this crusty old sea-dog? It's wasted on him promise you. Doesn't know nainsook from nunsveiling. Did your father send you to do the polite to the lord of the manor? My poor girl! You have all my sympathy. No wonder friend Piers was loth to unbar to me. Keeping you all to himself. Permit me to inform you, cousin, that I've been first-oars with *all* the Longden girls ever since I cut my wisdoms and I'll not have you stealing a march on me in this underhand manner."

He offered to escort Clemency home when she was ready to leave and exclaimed in horror on hearing that she had walked all that way. A very slight detour from his intended route would permit him to take her up in the gig, "And Betsy, too, for you'd not be without your watchdog would you, Miss Clee?" He then added in an audible aside to his cousin, "There you are, my lad. That's how it's done. As neat a cutting out operation as ever you've seen at sea. Let that be a lesson to you!"

Clemency said that Betsy would be dreadfully cross at being kept waiting so long, whereupon Giles advised his cousin not to risk a brush with the formidable Miss Love if that was her mood. "Our Betsy-love is a bit of a tartar when roused to ire, but I am quite one of her favourites and may hope to escape with a mild scold. She would have *you* reduced a quivering jelly inside two minutes."

Piers directed a glance that would have quelled a mutiny at his irrepressible cousin and ignored the kind advice, performing the necessary courtesies with a grave air that lent them a touch of old world chivalry. Miss Love, studying him with a critical regard that she made no attempt to conceal, found him quite a personable young man. Further than that she would not commit herself until she saw how he dealt with her darlings. Piers, for his part, met her fierce scrutiny with outward composure despite his guilty conscience. Viewing the wrinkled old face and noting its doting fondness as the faded eyes turned to the girl at his side, he was thankful that Mistress Love did not know that she had cause for complaint against him far more serious than the minor inconvenience of being kept waiting.

He informed Clemency that he would certainly do himself the honour of calling upon her Papa at an early date, a remark that caused her to open her eyes in surprised fashion but earned a nod of what might almost pass for approval from Betsy, and watched the gig bowl away.

His hearing was acute — the air very still. Clearly across the intervening space he heard Giles say, "Now, young Clee. You've been up to mischief, I know. Confession please." With a wry little grin he wondered how far confession would go.

Chapter Three

WHEN Piers put in an appearance at his aunt's dinner table that night it was to find that Miss Longden's morning call was the main topic of conversation. Perhaps the girl had felt bound to give some explanation of her unorthodox behaviour. At any rate she had spoken quite openly of the reason for her visit.

Giles was outraged, declaring that he had never heard anything so preposterous, and trusting that his cousin had scotched so crazy a start at the very outset. But before Piers could explain that he had done just that, Lady Eleanor struck a doubting note.

"I cannot believe that Clemency would have made such an approach unless the case had been really desperate," she said gravely. "For a child so gently bred to have taken so reckless a step, to approach one who is all but a stranger, she must indeed have been hard driven. One cannot help being aware that the Longdens have been in very straitened circumstances this past year, and lately I have heard hints that John is deeply involved in this South American business. Naturally they never plead poverty, but it is perfectly obvious that it is make and scrape with them. None of the girls has had a new gown since I don't know when."

"Well, Clee was wearing a very smart rig this morning." retorted Giles. "As fine as fivepence in silk and velvet, and feathers in her hat."

"*Clemency* was?" exclaimed his mother in horrified accents. "In the morning? In the country? Oh! Indeed something is very much amiss. Is this really true, Piers?"

Her nephew grinned. "The young lady was certainly very *expensively* clad," he acknowledged, "but not, I would say, fashionably. Indeed I was left with the impression that bonnet and dress had been made for an older lady. The bonnet, in particular, was too large for its wearer," and he could not restrain a soft chuckle at the memory.

"This is no laughing matter," declared Lady Eleanor indignantly. "She must have been wearing some of her Mama's things, and if that is indeed the case, then matters are serious." And she proceeded to outline to her nephew the awkward state of affairs in the Longden household.

It seemed to him impractical to the point of farce that the family should be living in circumstances of some privation when there was money to be obtained easily enough by the sacrifice of some stupidly sentimental scruples, and he said so, in somewhat forthright fashion.

"You don't understand, dear," said his aunt tolerantly. "The girls worship their father — and I'm sure it's no wonder, for he is quite the kindest parent any daughter could desire — and so brave in his affliction." She broke off as a wrinkle of distaste curled her nephew's mouth, and said sharply, "No. Not at all what you are thinking. Not cheap dramatics brave. There is no heroic posing to catch sympathy. It is just that he has overcome his difficulties to the point that you would scarcely know that he *was* blind."

"Blind, is he, poor devil?" said Piers soberly. "I did not know — though all of you kept referring to his affliction. I thought you meant the loss of his wife and the mystery surrounding her end, which is certainly trouble enough for any man."

Here Giles intervened to give a brief account of the incident which had brought tragedy to their neighbour — an all too familiar tale of careless folly — a youngster carrying a loaded gun and crossing a stone stile in shoes grown slippery on the soft turf. Piers nodded shortly. There would always be reckless fools, too set up in their own conceit to listen to experience.

"So you see how it is," pursued Lady Eleanor patiently. "His one fault, poor man, is his refusal to face up to the probability of his wife's death. And the girls shrink from forcing that acceptance upon him. But if they are brought so low as to be seeking employment, then something will *have* to be done. You must not blame John overmuch," she added fairly. "The girls have undoubtedly shielded him from the truth. Which is, alas, all too easily done. Now he will have to be told, but the question is — who is to do the telling?"

There was a tight little silence. The cousins looked at each other. Lady Eleanor, secure in the knowledge that neither of them would permit *her* to undertake so uncomfortable a task, considered them both thoughtfully. Piers, she decided inwardly, and not only to spare her son. Piers would do it better, impersonally yet kindly. Giles would stammer and hedge and embarrass his listener as deeply as himself. Even as she reached this decision, Giles spoke for her.

"All yours, cousin," he grinned, and went on reasonably enough. "In Longden's eyes I'm little more than schoolboy. What weight would my opinions carry? You're a man of the world — travelled — experienced. He might listen to you. He might even, in view of that old obligation, accept your help in sorting out his affairs."

Piers looked up sharply. Here again was the mention of an obligation. "Miss Longden mentioned something of the sort," he said slowly. "I was taken sadly at fault, for indeed I had no recollection of it, yet dare not confess my ignorance."

Lady Eleanor laughed. "How should you know, indeed? You were a mere babe at the time. But of course the Longden girls have been brought up on the story — just the sort of tale that nursemaids delight in. I daresay John has forgotten the incident as completely as you have. But I do see that it makes a difference," she went on thoughtfully. "Undoubtedly that is why Clemency felt that she might properly approach you." She nodded comfortably to herself, satisfied that her young friend had not, after all, so grossly transgressed the principles of her upbringing. Piers glanced from one to the other and demanded further enlightenment.

Giles obliged. "Yes, indeed, dear cousin. Only consider! If John Longden had not been so sure and cool a shot, I might well have fallen heir to all your worldly wealth. Though to be sure it would be a poor exchange for the pleasure of your society. Oh, yes —" for Piers was threatening dire punishment — "the tale is that he shot a mad dog just as it was about to sink its fangs into your infant person. None of the others dare shoot, for fear of hitting you."

An odd little frisson of horror chilled Piers's blood. He had once seen a man die of hydrophobia. Inured as he was to the hideous injuries so often incurred at sea, that was still not a memory that he cared to recall. He had never guessed how easily it might have been his own fate. He glanced down at the powerful brown fingers holding his wine glass and thought of the pleasure he had taken of life. No wonder the chit had spoken of an obligation. Willingly he would admit it. Rather less willingly would he broach the subject of insolvency to his benefactor. However it was clearly his duty, and he was not one to put off a distasteful task.

"I will call on him tomorrow," he said briskly. "I may be a little late in getting back from Otterley's, but not enough to signify. I hope Mr. Longden isn't a stickler for punctilio."

His aunt beamed approval at him. "Indeed he is not," she affirmed. "The least consequential of men. You will deal famously together. And it will be a great weight off my mind. I have been very anxious about those girls with only Betsy to turn to, and Clemency so fiery proud. The other two are more biddable, but Clemency is one who will always take her own way, however reckless, rather than depend on her elders. If you are to take them in charge I shall breathe more easily."

Giles nodded agreement. "Aye. She's a bit hot at hand is Mistress Clemency, but sound as a roast for all that. I warrant she'll be downright grateful for your counsel and support."

Piers thought they were both going a great deal too fast. He did not intend to involve himself deeply in the Longdens' affairs. He would explain the position to Mr. Longden, discover tactfully if a loan would be accepted, and rid himself of the awkward business as soon as his sense of obligation permitted. As for Miss Longden being grateful for his help, it seemed to him highly improbable after what had passed between them. He was determined to regard his mood of the morning as a temporary madness which he would learn to subdue in good time. There was no place for a woman in the life that he had chosen, certainly not for a frail, delicately bred child. Not even his wealth, and it was already considerable and still growing, since the Yorkshire manufacturers were buying up his cross-bred wool with an eagerness only exceeded by their enthusiasm for Macarthur's merino, could wrap a girl in comfort of the English standard in that far away colony. He said dryly that Miss Longden had not struck him as the kind of young lady who was eager to listen to good advice, and turned the subject by asking about some leases that Giles had been checking for him. Giles expounded at some length, and ended by asking if his cousin did not now wish to take matters into his own hands.

Piers shook his head. "I've no intention of settling here," he said bluntly, answering the question that had not found utterance. "Australia for me, with the Dower House as a second home when business brings me back. I've been meaning to discuss some such arrangement with you. If it suits, I'd have you take over here, Giles. The place will come to you in any case at my death. I'd rather see you enjoy it in my lifetime, and maybe," he grinned at his cousin, "a parcel of brats in your image to temper the enjoyment."

He sat patiently through the storm of protest that ensued. He had not expected to win his way at first asking. His aunt, while expressing her deep appreciation of his generous offer, deprecated his intention of residing abroad. Giles wanted to know if he reckoned him incapable of making his own way in the world. It would take time to bring them round to his point of view, but ultimately he would succeed. They were his family. Why should he not provide for them, who could so well afford to do so? But he did not put forward *this* argument, advancing instead several temperate observations on difficulties that arose when the landlord was an absentee. When he felt he had made sufficient headway he left them to think it over and discuss it in private, pleading his early start next day as his excuse for leaving betimes.

But despite the early start it proved impossible to hurry old Mr. Otterley in his careful inspection of the samples of wool. Each must be tested carefully in his fingers and then examined under a magnifying glass, so that it was past five o'clock before Piers found himself free to fulfil his promise to call at Ash Croft. Nevertheless he hesitated only briefly. The unpleasant interview had been on his mind all day. Even if the hour was unconventional, best tackle it now.

He trod up a sadly neglected drive between untrimmed hedges to the front door. The house looked forlorn, with ivy encroaching on stonework where it should never have been permitted. There was no trace of smoke from the chimneys. All the evidence suggested that Miss Longden's tale of poverty had actually been understated, and he was uneasily aware that his judgement had been less than fair. He tugged roughly at the bell pull, releasing some of his annoyance. He could hear the bell jangling in the distance but it was some time before footsteps could be heard approaching. There was the rattle of a chain and a struggle with a stiff bolt and then Betsy's crabbed visage peered at him suspiciously round the edge of the door as though she suspected him of being a house breaker or a debt collector. Recognition dawning, she set the door wider but still stood foursquare in his path making no attempt to invite him to enter.

Between amusement and irritability he enquired if it would be convenient for Mr. Longden to receive him. It was, he admitted, an odd time to be paying a call, but his business was urgent and his time limited.

Betsy must have reached a favourable decision for she accorded him a brisk nod, muttered something that sounded like, "No time better," and stood aside to allow him to enter the dark hall.

"Ye'll need to mind that wall," she instructed him gruffly. "There's stags' heads and suchlike. Don't go bumping into them. Keep to this side and you'll be all right."

He wondered why there was no lamp burning to make the warning unnecessary as he followed his guide along a murky passage and nearly stumbled over her as she stopped unexpectedly to tap on a door. Of course a blind man had no need of lamps, but surely the daughters didn't creep about in this gloom?

At least there was a glimmer of light in the room into which the old servant was ushering him, with a curt, "Captain Kennedy to see you, Sir." It came from a single candle set on the table, and Piers realised with dismay that his call had interrupted the family at dinner. But his stammered apology was swept aside by his host who rose to greet him with every appearance of sincere welcome.

"Nonsense, my dear boy, I'm delighted," exclaimed the blind man, advancing confidently with outstretched hand. "Pru, set another place for our guest. I can recommend the game fricassee," he went on hospitably. "Some of your own birds that young Giles sent down. Of course you must stay. I'll take no refusal. We always dine early — one gets so devilish sharp-set in the country. Your aunt will forgive you for once — you can tell her it was all my blame. She'll understand that the chance of masculine support was one that I couldn't resist, petticoat-ridden as I am," and he smiled at his daughters with pride and love. "You'll not remember my girls. Clemency, my eldest, and Prudence, younger by a quarter of an hour, and Faith, my baby. Make your curtsies to Captain Kennedy, my dears. Put him next to me, Pru. No need for ceremony, we're old acquaintances, though it must be close on twenty years since last we met."

The tall girl had risen and was bringing cutlery from a side table. Clemency had been seated with her back to him but had swung round at the interruption, and she and the younger girl were staring at him with such expressions of shocked dismay that he began to wonder if there was something amiss with his appearance. His host, still in a bustle of hospitality, was directing Faith to set a chair for the unexpected guest, and asking Clemency if they had any of the good port left — the '75 — for this was an occasion and should be duly celebrated.

Piers's eyes had now accustomed themselves to the dim light. A glance at the table with its snowy damask and gleaming silver showed him the true cause of the horror stricken faces. There was certainly a dish which had presumably contained the fricassee of game, but its entire contents were on Mr. Longden's plate. The girls were eating baked potatoes.

He looked swiftly at Clemency, erect as a lance in her chair at the foot of the table. Her head was high, but the great brown eyes were full of shamed tears. He found her distress unbelievably painful, the more so by contrast with the gallant front she had shown at their first meeting. He turned back to his host. "It smells wonderful, Sir," he said, and smiled delightfully. "I shall certainly allow myself to be tempted. Thank you, Miss Prudence. Shall I serve myself?" And did so, helping himself to a potato from the dish which still held several.

Prudence flashed him a glance glowing with gratitude, picked up the empty meat dish and made a slight clatter with spoon and fork before removing it to the side table. The action was so practised, so automatic, that Piers realised that this scene had been played many times before. Pitifully he remembered Clemency's surprising greed over the cakes. No wonder, if the poor little brat was half starved. It was difficult to suppress his burning indignation, which, he discovered, was directed mainly at himself. Only the need to maintain a courteous interchange with his host saved him. When Betsy appeared with a dish of baked apples he was thankful to see that at least the girls shared *this* treat, though he declined it for himself, saying that he was not yet accustomed to country hours and that having done such ample justice to the first course, dare not indulge further greed. A statement which so moved Betsy that she actually patted his shoulder with possessive approbation before retiring to her kitchen fastness.

Faith was gazing at him with blatant adoration, Prudence smiling over Betsy's open capitulation, but Clemency remained stony faced, speaking only when directly addressed. If Giles had not appeared so untimely, she might, he thought, have forgiven him those stolen kisses. She would find it much harder to forgive him for having discovered the depth of their poverty. The delicate veil that she had drawn over it had been brutally wrenched aside by Betsy's meddling. He could not be sorry that the truth had been shown him — but he knew, ruefully, who would be blamed.

The travesty of a meal was almost done, and his hostess, at least, would not press him to stay longer. With his host he now wished to avoid intimate talk until he felt his way a little more clearly. The position was more serious and more delicate than he had guessed. He could picture John Longden's distress if he should ever discover that his daughters had taken advantage of his blindness to starve themselves while he lived well. He excused himself to his host, saying that his aunt might be growing anxious over his non-appearance, and asked him to name a convenient date when they would all dine with him at the Dower House. "Though I fear Mrs. Beach can produce nothing so good as your fricassee," he added. Mr. Longden beamed his delight.

"You are complimenting my cook to her face," he exclaimed. "Clemency made it."

And he had advised the girl to study domestic economy! He was thankful when his host told Prudence that she might set up the chess board for their usual game and then escorted him to the door.

His farewells done, he walked briskly to the gate. But having made his departure perfectly audible, in view of Mistress Prudence's by-play with plates and cutlery, he paused to consider his next move. If Prudence and her father were playing chess, it seemed to him very likely that Clemency would repair to the kitchen quarters, if not to help Betsy with domestic tasks, then certainly to scold her for admitting him into their carefully guarded secret.

He allowed the chess game time to be well under way before climbing the gate, lest its creaking betray him, and fetching a wide circle round the house. A lighted window led him to the kitchen, but no one answered his soft tap although he could hear voices inside. This was no time for standing on ceremony. By conniving at the deception he had joined the conspirators. He lifted the latch and walked in.

Chapter Four

THE scene was much as he had expected. Betsy was standing on the hearth, arms akimbo and an obstinate jut to her chin. Faith, flushed and excited, broke off what she was saying to stare at his sudden appearance. Clemency was sitting at the kitchen table, her head buried in her arms, one clenched fist beating a fierce tattoo on the scrubbed deal, and did not see him.

Betsy nodded to him as though it was quite customary to have strange men stroll into her kitchen unannounced, then jerked her head significantly towards the table.

"So it's you, is it?" she grunted. "I reckoned you'd be back. And a fine mess of trouble we're in, you and me, with her ladyship here."

Clemency's head came up at that. Piers had feared that she was crying. Now that he saw the white furious face and blazing eyes he realised that she was only in a tearing rage. "Fiery proud", Aunt Eleanor had said, and Gad! She looked it! A regular hell-cat, ready to spit and claw at the least provocation. He was thankful. Tantrums, he felt, would be easier to handle than tears.

She was on her feet and coming at him, a small virago without fear or diffidence. "How dare you burst in here without knocking?" she hurled at him. "Another sample of your polished manners I suppose! You can just take yourself off as quickly as you please. You have found out all you wished to know and now you may leave us to manage our affairs without your interference."

Piers smiled at her kindly. "Thank you, my child," he said. "I will indeed take myself off just as soon as I please. That will not be until you and I have reached a better understanding. And if you must rant at me like a fishwife, lower your voice. Do you want your father to hear you and come seeking the cause of the rumpus?"

That had checked the first onslaught. Now for a little soothing balm to lay the ruffled feathers. "I came to apologise to you. And actually I *did* knock, but no doubt you were too engrossed to hear me. I am truly sorry that I did not treat your request more seriously yesterday morning. I did not

35

understand the full extent of your difficulties. You looked so very prosperous and fashionable, you see, and not in the least like a young lady seeking work. And I was *not* aware of my deep obligation to your father until my aunt explained it to me. Since it appears that I was only two at the time, perhaps you will consent to overlook this fault in me, for had I perfectly understood all the circumstances my answer must have been very different. I came here tonight for no other purpose than to explain this, and to beg the privilege of serving you. I had no intention of intruding on you privacy."

That last bit threw the blame for his disastrous intrusion wholly on poor Betsy, but since she was nodding approval at him from her stance on the hearth he didn't suppose she minded. The ruffled plumage seemed to be subsiding. Faith caused a slight setback by suddenly exclaiming.

"Well *I* think you're perfectly sweet, and I can't imagine why Clemency said you were a surl —" and then clapped a hand to her lips in comical dismay.

Piers smiled at her. "A surly old curmudgeon?" he enquired amusedly. "I'm afraid your sister was in the right of it, Miss Faith. My behaviour was very bad. There can be nothing more painful than being treated as a foolish child when your trouble is real and serious. Stand my friend with her, and beg her to forgive me and permit me to help you in any way I can."

Faith's worshipping eyes were answer enough. Clemency said coldly, "I accept your explanation, Captain Kennedy and will absolve you of any intention of prying on us tonight. I cannot, however, bring myself to accept help which is clearly dictated by charitable motives, so I will bid you good night once more."

She should feel better now, after such a masterly set-down, decided Piers cheerfully. It was time to return to the attack.

"Certainly I will leave you, if you insist, Miss Longden," he said politely. "It seems only fair, however to warn you that if I do, I shall go straight to your father and tell him the whole truth."

Colour flared in the icy little face. "You *would* not!" she exclaimed. "Not even *you* could be so mean, so base!"

"Oh, yes I could! You are already aware that I do not subscribe to the gentlemanly code. I am a rough colonial, and when I fight I use any weapons to hand. And in this particular contest I am wholly set on emerging the victor."

He certainly looked it, though a close observer might have thought the determined mouth belied by a certain twinkle in the blue eyes. Clemency was too aghast to notice such details, but there was an answering gleam in Betsy's eye. So Mistress Clemency had met her master at last. She smoothed a gnarled hand over twitching lips to conceal her amusement.

He did not want the spunky little thing to have to admit defeat, so how to contrive an opening that would allow her to concede gracefully?

"You will not deny me the right to serve your father? Why, when he shot that rabid brute he gave me my life deliberately, so that in a sense he is my father too. You would not refuse me the privileges of a son?"

There came a shade of doubt into the fierce little face. He was clearly on the right tack. Now for a shattering broadside.

"I will solemnly promise you that there shall be no question of charity. Any arrangements that we are able to contrive shall be on a business footing. It may be necessary, as a temporary measure, for you to accept a trifling loan, since it is scarcely possible to find the sort of work that you require at a moment's notice. But you shall repay every penny, and a proper legal agreement to that effect shall be drawn up by your own man of business if you so prefer it."

That ought to hold her. Surely it sounded pompous enough to convince such an innocent. He had a sudden qualm. Ought he to have mentioned interest? Surely she would never have heard of anything so sordid? He must take care to rehearse that lawyer thoroughly in his part of the business.

"Very well," she said at last, reluctantly. "It shall be as you wish." And then, having swallowed the bitter pill, added with a change of front so complete that it left him speechless, "And I will even allow it to be a comfort to have someone else to do the worrying and contriving for a change. And you won't tell Papa, will you?" This last in so confiding and coaxing a tone that he could scarcely believe his ears.

"Not about the way you have all been deceiving him about the food," he promised gravely. "But we must consult him before we make any other arrangements. And that business of half starving yourselves is to stop at once," he added firmly. "I rely on you, Mistress Love, to see to that for me," and looking Betsy straight in the eye, explained solemnly, "You must not permit your young ladies to play such tricks with their health. No one would wish to employ sickly girls, so you must see that they keep well and strong."

"Yes, Sir," agreed Betsy with enthusiasm. "And my name is Betsy, Sir, since seemingly you're by way of being one of the family now."

Piers gravely thanked her for the privilege.

"There is just one other matter that should be put in hand at once. It is of some delicacy, and as a more man I would not presume to mention it, had its importance not already been proved to me." He cast down his eyes modestly. It helped, so new to lying as he was. "It will not do, I fear, to wear your fashionable silks when seeking employment. Your dress should be becoming — to be dowdy is quite as bad as being too smart — but it must be sensible and warm, evidence of your practical good taste. I beg your pardon for my plain speaking on this head, but it is my duty as your — er — adopted brother," — he avoided Betsy's eye — "to advise you to the best of my ability."

The idea was received better than he had dared to hope, and a further suggestion that Aunt Eleanor might help them choose suitable gowns was received with enthusiasm. He did not think it wise to press further help on them at the moment. Moreover, not being practised in the arts of the dissimulator, he felt that his ingenuity was giving out. However he reckoned that both Betsy and Aunt Eleanor would cheerfully conspire with him to keep prices low and commodities plentiful, so that the burden of debt should not sound too frightening. And the girls were only coming by their just deserts if he deceived them a little for their own good. After all, they had served the same trick on their father.

He bade them good night, reminding his 'sisters' that they were coming to dine with him on Saturday when they would be able to make further plans, whereupon Faith flung her arms round him and hugged him vigorously, vowing that he was a positive lamb and just the kind of brother that she would have chosen, had she been asked, unladylike behaviour which later called down upon her heedless head a severe lecture from her sister.

"For he is not really your brother, and it is most improper in you to treat him with such familiarity. Such conduct will scarcely recommend you as a responsible young lady seeking respectable employment." scolded Clemency, resolutely banishing from her mind certain vagaries in her own conduct where Captain Kennedy was concerned. After which a wholly unrepentant Faith danced off to see if the game of chess had come to an end, and whether there was any chance of imparting the exciting news to Prudence.

Chapter Five

THERE was a note from Lady Eleanor on the breakfast table next morning. One of the grooms had brought it over very early, said Betsy. She made no mention of a small package delivered to her by the same messenger, along with a verbal message that Captain Kennedy hoped that she would be able to make good use of the Australian seasoning that they had spoken of the previous evening. Betsy had glared at the groom with deep suspicion but it was clear that he knew nothing of the real nature of the package since he enquired with innocent interest as to whether she would use the herbs for dressing meat. She snubbed him smartly, declaring that she was not one for giving away her secrets to any chance enquirer, and bestowed the package carefully in the wooden spice box that held her cloves and coriander seeds.

When the abashed groom had taken his departure she bolted the door behind him and investigated the package. It held a sum of money in gold and bank notes that would keep them all in comfort for a considerable time. The spice box seemed as good a hiding place as any. She unscrewed the bottom section and by folding the notes into a tight wad fitted the precious hoard into its new resting place and put the box back on its high shelf.

"Australian seasoning indeed! Australian sauce-box, more likely! Though to be sure gold has been known to season many an unpalatable dish, so maybe he's in the right of it at that."

Lady Eleanor's note was an offer to take the girls shopping that very afternoon. Her nephew, she said, had told her of their wish to seek employment, and while she felt bound to deprecate such a course he had managed to convince her of its necessity. He had also suggested that they might do him a service by looking first at the cloth manufactured by a Mr. Otterley, with whom he had extensive business dealings. If they should chance to find anything suitable among Mr. Otterley's goods, Piers would be grateful to have personal reports on their wearing qualities. She did not add that she and Piers had racked their brains for an age before devising this scheme which would, they hoped, leave all details of price and payment in their hands.

Prudence was quite amenable. A new gown, whatever its source, was not to be sneezed at. Faith was puzzled as to how an officer in the navy came to have dealings with a woollen manufacturer, and Clemency was grimly determined that they would oblige the man who had overborne her natural independence. They would find something suitable among Mr. Otterley's fabrics however hideous their colours or coarse their quality.

Fortunately feminine instinct was not subjected to so severe a trial. After a brief interval of gloating irresistible after such long deprivation, they settled to the serious business of choice. Shopping at a warehouse was strange and new. The young man who had met them at the gate and escorted them to the pattern room was delighted to explain everything, telling them that the huge rolls of cloth held as much as sixty or seventy yards apiece, and giving them small samples to handle so that they might get the 'feel' of the goods, but an enquiry about price from the eldest Miss Longden seemed to nonplus him, and he rubbed his chin reflectively.

"Well, now," he began, his careful speech lapsing into a more natural dialect, "we don't sell short lengths, and you'll not be wanting a whole roll — less it's to fit out an orphanage or such — but there's short sample lengths, 'bout five or six yards that the boss thought might suit your needs. They come a bit cheaper, 'cos they're last year's designs," he ended glibly, remembering his instructions.

They ended by selecting a kerseymere, light but warm and soft enough to drape well. Prudence chose a deep rose colour, while Faith, who vowed she didn't want to wear pink ever again, chose green. Clemency was hesitating between the green, which she preferred, and a snuff brown which she thought would make her look older and more staid, when Lady Eleanor held up one of the small clippings and said, "How about this, my dear? It picks up the lighter tones in your hair quite beautifully."

It was a deep rich amber, and Clemency had already seen and coveted it, but there did not seem to be any more of it in the room. Upon enquiry the young man reflected judicially for several minutes before finally pronouncing, "Yes. I remember that piece, ma'am. Not a good seller. Difficult colour to wear for most ladies. Bound to be plenty of it left. I'll just see," and excused himself thankfully, mopping his brow in relief once he was out of the room and thanking heaven that his duties did not normally call for such equivocation.

Reporting to her nephew that night, Lady Eleanor assured him that the plan had worked splendidly; that the girls had not a notion of the way in which they had been tricked, and had accepted without a blink both the absurdly low price which had been quoted and the notion that five yard sample pieces were a commonplace in the wool trade. Clemency had turned awkward over the suggestion that they should get a seamstress to make up the dresses, "though it would cost only three or four shilling apiece," and had said that was an unnecessary expense when she and Faith were quite capable of doing the work themselves.

Piers laughed. "Good luck to the pair of them. Keep them out of mischief for a while. But I'd give a crown to have seen young Otterley's face. He's their prize salesman and it must have gone dead against the pluck to have to decry his goods."

"At least it cost him nothing — either in hard cash or goodwill," said his aunt dryly. "Piers — are you sure you can stand all this nonsense? What with wishing to make over a perfectly good estate to Giles, and now taking the Longdens under your protection, you are like to find yourself without a feather to fly with. I fell in with your plan today for those poor girls really needed warm dresses and I would willingly have paid for them myself. But I cannot for the life of me see why you did not explain the position to John, as was your intention, and why there has to be all this conspiracy. Felicity Longden had jewellery that would keep the family in comfort until the girls marry. Her emeralds, I know for a fact, were extremely valuable, and there were a number of other costly pieces. I really do not see why you should shoulder the responsibility."

"My dear aunt, I may not be a Croesus yet, but I assure you I shall not outrun the constable. Besides —" he grinned — "my trifling outlay is only a loan, to be repaid by Mistress Clemency out of her salary when she finds employment. I regard it as a very sound investment!"

His eyes were crinkled in mischievous enjoyment. Lady Eleanor said severely, "Now, Piers, you're not to tease the child. She's a wilful little piece, but she has been very awkwardly placed, and she is pluck to the backbone, as Giles would say."

"Giles has an interest there?" her nephew asked lazily.

"Goodness, no! He has a pronounced tendre for the other one — Prudence. They will suit very well. She is a sweet dispositioned girl and will make a good wife, besides inheriting a comfortable fortune some day

41

under the terms of her grandfather's deed of trust. But Giles is in no position to marry at present."

"All the more reason why he should make up his mind to taking over here," Piers pointed out, unaccountably pleased to discover that it was not Clemency who was the object of Giles's affections. "I am perfectly serious, you know, when I say that I shall never reside here permanently. I'm fond enough of the place, but it has never held me as it does you and Giles. My longing was all for the sea. And in some way that I find difficult to put into words my vast unknown country has taken the place of the sea. It holds the same kind of charm for me — wild, free, challenging. And richly rewarding." He laughed at his aunt's serious expression, a little shamefaced at having opened his heart so far and seeking to return to a more prosaic plane. "*Very* richly rewarding, dear aunt. I promise you, Giles need have no scruples about stepping into my shoes, and I have sufficient affection for the place and its people to wish to see them well served. Giles will do *that* to admiration."

His aunt shook her head, but she did not break into instant remonstrance as she had done when first he broached the idea. Satisfied, he turned the subject by asking if she would play hostess for him on Saturday evening as he had invited the Longdens to dinner. "And Giles, too, of course. I shall then have the opportunity of studying him *vis-à-vis* his Prudence. For once in my life I shall really feel like the head of the family."

She agreed to it willingly, only hoping that those poor girls had something fit to wear on such an occasion. "And you had better prepare yourself for being very relentlessly quizzed by the youngest Miss Longden," she informed him. "She's deep in the throes of hero worship and absolutely consumed with curiosity about you. No need to tell you that she is very young for her age and quite unaware of any impropriety in saying exactly what comes into her head."

"Young Faith?" grinned Piers indulgently. "She's a nice little soul. And about as fit to be thrown on the world as a new born lamb. What she really needs is to spend a year with a family who move in good circles. One with girls of her own age, where she could learn how to conduct herself in society. She's a pretty child and might well find herself a creditable husband. Now how could we arrange that, Aunt Eleanor?"

Fortunately for his aunt, who felt that, fond as she was of the Longdens, she had really heard enough of them for one day, dinner was announced and the problem was temporarily shelved.

The girls who had just been so thoroughly discussed were hard at work. The new dress lengths having been duly fondled and held up to three eager faces to see how well the colours suited had been laid aside, though an animated discussion was still in progress as to the styles in which they should be made up. Meanwhile three pairs of hands were busily furbishing up their dresses for Saturday night. Clemency had decreed that they should wear their muslins, countering Pru's shiver and mutter of, "Muslins — in October!" with an assurance that the Dower House was beautifully warm, and adding that nothing would persuade her to wear Mama's clothes again after her first disastrous essay. Carefully starched and ironed, the muslins would do well enough. Pru could wear Mama's Norwich shawl. She and Faith would wear spencers cut from the skirts of grandma's poplins. It was upon this task that they were engaged, while Prue painstakingly hemmed a ruffle designed to lengthen Faith's muslin which showed her ankles.

Sewing did not silence Faith's chatter. "I can't think why you took Captain Kennedy in such dislike, Clee. He's so handsome — so tall, and being tanned makes his eyes look bluer. And that white lock in his hair is positively romantic. I'm sure there's a story behind that. Perhaps he was wounded at Trafalgar." Her eyes shone, and her sewing dropped forgotten in her lap.

"Since he must have been about twelve years old when Trafalgar was fought, it seems improbable," said Clemency dryly, "unless he was serving as a powder monkey or a cabin boy, which seems equally unlikely. As for my taking him in dislike, it is no such thing. You heard him apologise for treating me as though I was a silly child. You could not expect me to like *that*. And if you neglect your sewing to talk about him, you will present a very odd appearance on Saturday night."

Whereupon Faith plied her needle with renewed industry, and the fascinating subject was allowed to drop.

Chapter Six

PIERS made no attempt at a formal dinner party. Even if his numbers had been even he had not the staff to deal with such an affair. And indeed a homely, 'family' type of party was more to his taste. After years of the strict etiquette observed in the Navy, he had discovered in himself a marked preference for simpler colonial ways.

He also had the innate tact to reject any thought of an elaborate meal which could only serve to remind three of his guests of a very different dinner table, though he *had* ordered a variety of creams and sweetmeats that he thought would be a treat for the girls without being too ostentatious.

The party went well from the beginning. The home made spencers had turned out successfully so the girls were able to feel themselves quite appropriately dressed, and Clemency had been much touched when Papa, just before leaving home, had produced a pearl necklace and said that he was sure that Mama would wish to lend it to her for the party. He clasped it about her throat himself, explaining to her sisters that most of Mama's jewellery was too grand and sophisticated for such very young ladies to wear, or they, too, should have had some pretty trinket to trick out their party dresses.

Conversation at first was a little shy and correct, except for the youngest guest, who found just the opportunity for which she had been waiting in the more restrained mood of her elders. Then her naïve and eager questioning elicited the fact that Captain Kennedy had once met Matthew Flinders.

That brought Clemency into the conversation, for the distinguished explorer was one of her heroes. Cheeks delicately flushed, brown eyes aglow, she quite forgot her fixed intention of treating her host with cool civility and poured out question after eager question. "Worse than Faith!" as Prudence told her when they talked the party over during the nightly hair brushing session. Her loving, detailed knowledge of those early voyages, especially that of the *Tom Thumb* quite amazed Piers, who had not thought that such matters would interest a girl.

"She ought to have been a boy. Then she could have run away to sea and gone a-roving herself," teased her father proudly, and broke the spell of self-forgetfulness. She realised that she had been monopolising her host, blushed, and turned back to her father to help him prepare a slice of pineapple. The easy, unobtrusive way in which the girls steered him through any small difficulty was a pleasant sight, thought Lady Eleanor, and drew Faith's attention to a lemon cream which had so far escaped her notice.

The three men moved closer together when the ladies had withdrawn and talked companionably over their wine. The talk turned again to Australia, Mr. Longden being particularly interested in the discoveries made the previous year when Howell and Hume had crossed the Murray river. Presently Piers suggested that his cousin might care to join the ladies as he wished to seize the opportunity of a private word with Mr. Longden, and Giles, nothing loth, went off to be warmly welcomed in the drawing-room, though one young lady at least was more concerned about the conversation that might be taking place downstairs.

The awkward moment being upon him, Piers tackled the problem with characteristic forthrightness.

"Sir, I am about to take outrageous advantage of my position as your host to introduce a subject rarely discussed between even the most intimate of friends — money."

Longden stiffened a little, though his expression of courteous attention remained unchanged.

Piers went on, "I have too high a regard for you to subscribe to the belief that one should hide unpleasant facts just because you have the misfortune to be blind. My aunt and your daughters seem to think this shielding is necessary. For myself, I imagine there is nothing you would like less."

The interrogative note in his voice received a crisp affirmative.

"Very well. Forgive my bluntness, but it is fairly generally known among your friends that you are in some financial difficulty because of the failure of these South American mines. You are not alone, of course. A great many fortunes have come to grief. But in your case, your daughters have hit upon the notion of helping you out of your difficulties by seeking situations."

There was a sharp exclamation of disbelief from the quiet man beside him.

"Quite true, Sir. Miss Longden called upon me last week to enlist my aid in forwarding the scheme. Not knowing the facts, I advised her to consult my aunt, and when she declined to do so, I told her and am sure you will subscribe to my view — that a man prefers to support his own daughters."

"Yes, indeed," said Longden simply. "Believe me truly grateful. Not for your disclosures, which are sufficiently unpalatable, but for having the courage and honesty to tell me the truth. Why must well meaning friends endeavour to shelter me from all unpleasantness? The pity is that it's so damned easy to do," he said bitterly, and then smiled in Piers's direction. "At least I can acquit you on that charge. Thank you for recognising that I am still a man."

"Why, thank you, Sir, for taking my interference in such good part," returned Piers, laughing a little. "I half expected you to damn me to hell for impudence."

Longden joined in the laughter, but sobered soon enough. "The case is this," he said ruefully. "Most of my personal fortune is sunk in those wretched mines. I should have left well alone. No head for business — never had. But I shall come about easily enough. I hold certain assets that will relieve the situation. I was loth to part with them, but rather than have my girls seeking their bread with strangers —" He broke off with a shrug of distaste.

"That is good hearing, Sir," said Piers politely. "If I can be of service to you, I beg you will not hesitate to make use of me. As you must be aware, I would be only too pleased to be able to repay in some small part my debt to you."

"Debt?" said Longden, puzzled. "I do not know of any — Good God! Not *that* old tale! You owe me nothing, boy. Had I been a little older and realised the risk I ran of hitting *you* rather than the dog, I had probably held my fire."

"Thank heaven you didn't. Better to have fired and hit me than leave me to risk so foul a death. I reckon myself very much obliged to you, and would be glad of the chance to prove it."

The older man smiled at him. "If you insist. I would be very well pleased to use you in this business, not one I would care to entrust to strangers. It is a matter of selling jewellery, and will, I imagine, entail a journey to London, or to some other large centre where such valuables may readily find a purchaser."

Piers mulled this over thoughtfully. Then he said, "I should think that, just at the present, with so many businesses tottering to ruin and even the banks in difficulties, jewellery would be a very sound investment. You could sell outright, or you could use it as security for negotiating a loan."

Mr. Longden sighed a little wearily. "Do as you think best, my boy. I have a slight prejudice against selling outright if any other means can be arranged, but I leave the decision to you. Perhaps we can discuss the business in more detail when you are at leisure."

That suited Piers very well, giving him a breathing space in which to perfect his plans. The amount of the 'loan' would have to be nicely calculated to support the family in decent comfort without being suspiciously lavish. It was not the time, when entertaining dinner guests, to apply himself to the fabrication of a tale that would serve. He was very happy to agree that further discussion should be deferred, and to offer his guest an arm to steer him to the drawing-room.

As they mounted the stairs, Longden said, suddenly, awkwardly, "You say that my difficulties are generally known. Is my poverty so very obvious?"

"Good God, no, Sir," lied Piers stoutly. "Just one or two small pointers. Putting down your carriage for instance, and selling your horses. Only your true friends would notice. And my aunt — women see these details — says that the girls are a trifle shabby." That would hurt, he knew, but it must be said if Longden was to realise the shifts to which his daughters had been put before they had been driven to the extreme course of seeking employment. At least he need not be told that they had gone hungry. He hastened to soothe the pain that he had inflicted by adding cheerfully, "I can assure you that they look very becomingly tonight. Your youngest promises to become a beauty. I make no doubt she will be all the rage when she makes her debut."

"Little Faith? She was always a taking child. But it is my Clemency who favours her mama. Not so pretty as her little sister, but a great-heart, loving and loyal to the last shred. But how shocking in me to be boring on for ever about my children. I beg your pardon. Of late we have gone about so little that I forget the observances of polite society."

"You should be thankful for it, Sir. Since I have made my home overseas I fear I find this business of social façade both false and wearisome. I much prefer an evening natural and gay, as tonight has been — if you discount our private talk — and shall hope to have the pleasure repeated frequently during my stay."

They entered the drawing-room at this point of amity, John Longden looking so cheerful that Clemency's tight clasped hands relaxed and her mouth curved in sympathy as she rose to take his hand and settle him in the chair that she had vacated by Lady Eleanor's side. The three younger members of the party were playing loo for cowrie shell stakes, and judging by the groans and the laughter getting as much fun out of it as if they had been playing for guineas.

"Shall we join these hardened gamesters?" invited Piers, but Clemency only shook her head.

"I would rather speak with you, Captain Kennedy, if I may do so without imposition."

He bowed, grave of countenance, if with an inward smile at her direct approach. "Then may I invite you to stroll in the conservatory for a while? A rather grandiose title for so small a place, and scant room for strolling, but it permits us to observe the conventions while affording a measure of privacy, which seems very desirable when you ask to speak with me in that minatory manner. I find myself instinctively recalling my latest sins and wondering which one has found me out."

She laughed at that, assured him that it was no such thing, and allowed him to lead her through the curtained entrance to the tiny conservatory which was Beach's private kingdom.

"Unusual in a sailor," commented Piers idly, "this passion for floriculture, but he has certainly made it a pleasant little place."

Clemency paid only courtesy attention to this opening gambit. "Sir, have you spoken to my father?" she demanded urgently.

"Yes, Miss Longden — upon the terms that we agreed. He is much opposed to your plan of seeking employment, and I would advise you to allow him to grow accustomed to the idea of so radical a change before making any further move in the matter. Meanwhile he intends to put his financial affairs in my hands. But you will appreciate that it would be most improper in me to discuss his intentions in detail, even with his daughter. No doubt he will tell you himself what he wishes you to know."

He could almost see the hackles rising and a decidedly militant glint in the brown eyes. He went on, with rueful amusement, "I suppose I am now equally involved with you in this conspiracy of deceit. Your father asked me point blank if his difficulties were so very patent. Are you shocked to hear that I lied to him as heartily as, I make no doubt, you would have done yourself?"

She softened visibly, even putting one slim hand on his sleeve in a gesture made up of apology and gratitude. "Thank you, Sir. That was kindly done." And then a mischievous smile curved that adorable mouth, and she said thoughtfully, "As a fellow conspirator you will find it rather more difficult to coerce me into submission, won't you? It is, after all, a game that two can play. How if I choose to destroy your credit with my father?"

He laughed down at her. "You won't do it, Miss Mischief, for your father's sake. Do you think I did not allow for that before so exposing myself to attack?"

With an impudence regrettable in a well brought up young lady she wrinkled her nose at him. He said softly. "If you do that again, my girl, I won't be answerable for the consequences. Don't rely too far on your privileged position as a guest in my house. I am already extremely desirous of repeating the shocking conduct to which I treated you at our first meeting. Don't tempt me too far."

She gasped, and coloured furiously, backing away towards the curtained doorway that led to safe chaperonage. He made no attempt to detain her, merely saying gently, "We shall now rejoin the rest of the party. But bear my warning in mind, Miss Longden, and never underrate your adversary, even if he is temporarily your ally."

Chapter Seven

THEY had scarcely done talking over the first party that they had attended in months, and the finishing touches had not yet been put to the new dresses, when Clemency found a temporary job.

The unwitting — not to say unwilling — cause of this sudden change of circumstance was Lady Eleanor. Setting forth briskly on her daily inspection of the dairy she had slipped on the blue flag pathway and fallen heavily. No serious damage was done, but she was badly shaken and further incapacitated by a sprained ankle and a dislocated thumb. The physician was cheerful, assuring her son that rest and a little cosseting would soon put matters to rights, and Lady Eleanor herself, enduring her discomforts with fortitude, assured her anxious menfolk that she would be perfectly well after a night's sleep. But next morning found her heavy eyed and feverish, while the nature of her injuries made it difficult for her to perform the smallest service for herself.

Piers, calling at Ash Croft and reporting this state of affairs, was promptly invited to carry Clemency and Faith back with him so that they might see what could be done to help their kind friend. He assented willingly, not mentioning several important business appointments, and enjoyed a private chuckle that Mistress Clemency did not propose to risk a *tête-à-tête* even when she was bound on an errand of mercy. Three was rather a tight fit in the curricle that he was driving on this occasion, especially when one of them carried a basket which in itself was quite a formidable chaperone. What in heaven's name could they be carrying to a house that was far better found than their own? Faith, who had now dispensed with all pretence of formality in her dealings with him, supplied the answer.

"Please drive steadily, won't you, Piers? There are eggs in the basket — our special brown ones — and if you overturn us they'll all be smashed, not to mention Betsy's things."

Further questioning elicited the information that Betsy had sent the invalid some of her famous herbal remedies, guaranteed to cure sprains and bruises far more efficiently than 'doctor's stuff' as their sender contemptuously described it. Then there was a comb of heather honey to which Lady Eleanor was extremely partial, and Faith was anxious that all these fragile treasures should arrive intact. "Though it is a great pity," she ended sorrowfully, "for I have never ridden in a curricle before, and I would love to go really fast."

Piers, overlooking the aspersion on his driving skill, meekly held the greys to a gentle trot, and managed to deposit both passengers and basket undamaged. He then took himself off at a spanking pace designed to make up for lost time, which caused Faith to gaze after him in wide-eyed admiration and Clemency to say that he was an odious show-off, on which head they wrangled amicably until they were admitted to Lady Eleanor's bedchamber.

They found her a little improved but restless and uncomfortable and glad to have her sheets and pillows smoothed and her face bathed by Clemency, while Faith moved quietly about the room tidying away various misplaced articles which had been infuriating the meticulously neat patient by their disorder.

"Oh! That is so much better," she sighed gratefully when they had settled her comfortably and sat down to chat. "So foolish of me to let such trifles fret me, but it is enough to drive one crazy, lying here helpless and the room in such a state. I found myself almost wishing that I had succumbed to Giles's persuasions to engage a personal maid. He wished me to do so, you know, last year when I was so low after the influenza, but it seemed to me a needless extravagance, with Mattie so neat fingered over hooking up my gowns and very obliging about setting a stitch where it is needed. And I have always preferred to keep my own room in order. You cannot imagine how much better I feel to see all tidy again. You are two dear good girls — and so is Prudence, for I make no doubt she would be here as well if it were not for caring for your papa."

"Indeed she would, ma'am, and has sent you some of her heather honey and the brown eggs that you prefer in token of her sympathy."

"Dear child," murmured Lady Eleanor fondly, and added rather inconsequently, "I cannot imagine why *our* hens never lay brown eggs, but the poultry woman assures me that they never do — and I expect she is perfectly to be trusted, do not you?"

Faith swallowed a giggle. The poultry woman was a contemporary and bitter rival of Betsy's. She had the face and disposition of a battle axe, and a fierce pride in her witless charges which only stopped short of *dyeing* their eggs brown to suit her fastidious mistress because she could see no way of doing it short of boiling them. The suggestion that she might be guilty of tampering with the manor's eggs was distinctly comical. Clemency was quite thankful when Lady Eleanor suggested that her little sister might care to go down to the stables to look at a new filly foal, just two days old, before Faith was betrayed into unbecoming mirth. When she was done in the stables, added their hostess, she might bring up some hot milk and queen cakes. It would spare the maids, and goodness knew what state of muddle they were all in below stairs, lacking her personal supervision.

Clemency assured her hostess that the household seemed to be running on oiled wheels, as was only to be expected with maids so well trained. "Besides," she added, "they are all perfectly devoted to you, and you may be sure they will all surpass themselves in their wish to help you get better." And seeing Lady Eleanor soothed and gratified by this remark, asked if she would not now like to rest a little.

"I am not at all tired," said Lady Eleanor firmly, as of long habit. "But if you could spare the time I would like it very much, my dear, if you would brush my hair for me. I would not ask it of you, but Mattie is not used to dressing hair, and though she braided it as best she could it feels just as though it is dragging my scalp off. And with this —" she indicated her bandaged hand — "I am so clumsy."

Mattie was the second housemaid, and more accustomed to brushing carpets than hair. Clemency helped the invalid remove her becoming cap and loosed the tight braids.

Out of a peaceful silence Lady Eleanor said sleepily. "You have a wondrous gentle touch. I could almost believe you were my daughter." And then, rousing a little, "It is at times such as this that one wishes for a daughter, to pet and cosset one as no paid servant could do. Though to be sure I was very thankful to have born my dear Sir John a son when Giles came."

Clemency smiled at her through the tall pier glass into which she was pensively gazing. "Well I certainly would not have *wished* you to have so uncomfortable an experience," she said, "but since it has happened it does at least give us the satisfaction of repaying a little of your kindness. If you remember, you would not have us near you when you were so poorly last year for fear that we would take the influenza too."

"At least there is no such danger with this complaint," said Lady Eleanor cheerfully, "and I shall be very well pleased to have you visit me whenever you can spare the time. But I won't have you walking all that way. Ask Giles to lend you Jenny and the gig. You will be quite safe. Dear Jenny is so gentle. I often drive her myself."

Clemency accepted the suggestion willingly and said that in that case she would drive over again in the evening and see her friend comfortably settled for the night. Lady Eleanor was rather doubtful about that. To be sure the hunter's moon was at the full and it was near as bright as day, but there had been nasty stories recently of highwaymen operating in the neighbourhood. Clemency only laughed at her. Even if the tales were true, such gentry would pay no attention to a female driving a gig. Lady Eleanor allowed inclination to overcome her natural caution and permitted herself to be overborne.

The entrance of Faith, carrying a tray and full of eager talk about the new foal and the choice of a name for the little creature swept away any lingering doubts as to the wisdom of the plan, and at the end of some twenty minutes devoted to refreshment and feminine chit-chat the sisters bade her good-bye and left her to rest, Clemency repeating from the threshold her promise to come again that evening.

As their voices faded — for they were arguing again, this time as to which of them should drive the placid Jenny — Lady Eleanor closed her eyes and relaxed against the pillows. She was not asleep — her mind was extremely active. Could her misfortune be turned to good account in furthering Piers's plans for helping the Longdens? But try as she would she could not work out any acceptable scheme. Clemency would be bitterly hurt if she were offered paid work where she had given loving kindness. And sick room tasks were menial, even if one dignified the post by calling it that of companion to an invalid. Besides she knew perfectly well that she would be up and active as soon as she could hobble about, not being of the temperament to prolong the role of fragile convalescent, even to oblige nephew Piers. She gave up teasing her brain and went to sleep.

When her menfolk strolled in at dusk to see how she did, they found her much brighter for the refreshing nap that she had enjoyed and ready to take an interest in life once more. Giles had brought a tight little posy of late blooming roses to cheer her sickroom, a graceful attention that caused her to decide that falling in love was a very *developing* thing for a young man, making him more sensitive to the needs and tastes of all womankind. She directed him carefully as to the bestowal of the roses, accepted with thanks the letters that her nephew had brought up from the receiving office, and proceeded to give them an animated account of her day. Presently Giles went off to change his dress for dinner. Piers, who had already exchanged breeches and driving jacket for the more formal pantaloons and cutaway coat suitable to attendance on an invalid lady, strolled across to the hearth and began methodically building up the fire while his aunt expounded to him her ponderings on the possibility of employing Clemency.

He heard her out thoughtfully, but shook his head. "I'm afraid you're right," he said regretfully. "It would be quite ideal — but it just wouldn't work. As for you playing *malade imaginaire* — well that wouldn't work either. You'd never stick it. And that girl's as sharp as she can hold together. She'd spot the fake in a trice. A pity — but no. Never fret, we'll think of something yet. By the way, I'm off to London tomorrow, on business for Mr. Longden, and expect to be gone the best part of a week. I have managed to defer some of my own engagements until I return, but it is going to be difficult to fit in all the visits I had planned. I may have to invite some of my clients to wait upon *me*, to save time. Would you have any objection to such a scheme?"

"Good gracious, no! How can you be so absurd! Anything that will ease your work can only be most acceptable to me."

He smiled down at her. "No objection that I smell of the shop? I do, you know, Aunt Nell. There is a wide gulf between the naval officer and a colonial sheep farmer and wool merchant. I might imperil your social standing."

"You do well to tease me so when I can neither come at you easily nor box your ears as you deserve," said his aunt indignantly. "Are you the less a gentleman for your dealings with the Longdens — with Giles? And what makes your generosity possible but the wool trade? You should be ashamed to despise the good fruits of your labours."

He stooped and hugged her hard and rather painfully, forgetting her bruises, and dropped a light kiss on her cheek. "My own sweet Aunt Nell. You're a darling — did you know? When I find a girl just like you, I'll have her over my saddle bow and be off to the far Antipodes before she can draw breath to say no. But alas! They do not breed them in your style today. They're all shrugs and sighs and artifice, and 'La! A farmer. How curious!' So you need not anticipate my immediate elopement. Don't look so distressed, love! I fare very well as a bachelor. Here — read your letters. I'll trim the lamp for you."

His aunt, aware that the brief moment of intimacy was over, feigned deep interest in her correspondence, a feigning that turned to reality as she picked up a letter addressed in a familiar hand and exclaimed joyously, "Chloe! And I have so wondered about them. They were up in Scotland, you know, with Huntley's parents, when Priscilla took the measles — and she turned sixteen! Of course the boys got them too, and even little Caroline. I do hope —" Further comment faded as she unfolded the crackling sheet. Piers smiled quietly into the fireglow. A letter from her sister would do more to raise Aunt Eleanor's spirits than any medicine.

Not so. There came a tragic wail from the bed. "Piers! Now we really *are* in the suds! They are coming here — all of them — and Nurse and Chloe's maid, and hope to be with us by the twenty-first. Why! That's less than a week away. What in the world shall I do? Who is to see to all the preparations? They hope to stay for a month at least, which is delightful of course, and as Chloe says no doubt it will set the boys up nicely. Gavin still has a nasty cough and I'm sure nothing could be more beneficial than our fresh country air. But I wasn't expecting them till next month. Oh! Piers!"

At that point she ran out of breath and thrust her hands up through her hair, setting her cap wildly askew and pressing her fingers to her temples as though to summon inspiration by sheer will power. And as seemed only proper in response to such desperate appeal, it came. She bounced erect, gave a wince of pain as her bruised ribs resented such energetic action, and beamed upon her nephew as together they exclaimed, "Clemency Longden."

"Now that is a truly excellent notion," said Piers. "She must perceive that the help is really needed and that you would certainly have to hire a temporary housekeeper under the circumstances. Naturally you would rather have a girl who knows your ways."

"But she will still wish to do it out of friendship," said his aunt gloomily.

"Yes, if you approach her directly," agreed Piers. "But we shall stage a little play for her benefit. When she comes to see you tonight, you and Giles shall be discussing the wording of an advertisement for this paragon who is so urgently needed. She will certainly volunteer her services, and then you must be very firm and say that nothing would suit you better but that it *must* be a business arrangement. And don't forget that a temporary post is always more highly paid than a permanent one."

Lady Eleanor lay back on her pillows and laughed. "You're an unprincipled wretch," she told him. "That poor child. It is a great shame to deceive her so, but I do believe it will take the trick."

Giles was called into consultation, the situation explained to him, and his part in the projected comedy limned in. At first impatient at the necessity for such artifice he was gradually cajoled into amusement and eventually to downright enthusiasm, though he still insisted that his cousin would play the part with more verve. Piers, knowing full well that, in such a context, his every utterance would be deeply suspect, pointed out that it was more natural for a son to help his mother in such domestic difficulties rather than a mere nephew, and Giles allowed himself to be convinced, even adding one or two touches of his own to the play, which, he declared, added credibility.

So it was that Clemency walked in upon a carefully rehearsed and well set scene. Giles, pocket book and pencil in hand, had fixed his mother with an attentive gaze and was saying, "Surely, Mama, five guineas is rather high?"

"Not at all, my dear. I happen to know that when Chloe was so ill after Caroline was born, they engaged a housekeeper at exactly that figure. One always has to pay higher for temporary help, and we need someone quite exceptional, someone who is sensible and capable but will not object to the incursion of a lively family."

At this point she chose to notice Clemency's arrival and held out both hands in anguished appeal. "Clemency! My love we are in *such* a fix! Chloe and the children are arriving in less than a week. Seven of them — and me —" she allowed histrionic fervour to overcome grammatical accuracy — "in this state! I was quite at my wits' end, I vow, until Giles insisted that we should advertise for a temporary housekeeper. And how we are to find anyone suitable in so short a time I simply cannot imagine."

It was really too easy, thought Giles guiltily. Clemency might have been as carefuly rehearsed in her part as they were themselves. Her offer of help came quite as spontaneously as Piers had anticipated, and the little scene played itself to a satisfactory conclusion with a still reluctant Clemency finally agreeing to accept a salary for her services and Giles thankfully tearing up some remarkably unconvincing notes.

Chapter Eight

CLEMENCY took up quarters at the Manor, since there was no time now to be wasted on driving to and fro, but Jenny and the gig were left at the disposal of her sisters and Faith came over nearly every day to see if she could make herself useful. Lady Eleanor had insisted that one of her own young maids should be lent to Betsy to help her with the rough work and so free the old woman for the tasks that had been Clemency's. Betsy, much gratified at having even one under servant, decided that times were on the mend at last. Privately, Lady Eleanor told Clemency that she was glad to get this particular girl away from the Manor for a while.

"She is Grant's daughter, you know, from the West Lodge, and a sensible willing girl. But it seems that she was much attached to that ne'er-do-well cousin of hers, Will Overing, and the news that he has run off from the White Swan where Grant had found him a place in the stables has upset her. I suspect that the other girls tease her about her runaway gypsy sweetheart, and make no doubt that she too will be glad of the change. Betsy's tongue may be sharp and she will make Elspeth work hard, but under the crust she is a motherly soul and will be kind to the girl."

By the end of her own first day at work, Clemency had discovered that her job was no sinecure; that she really was earning some, at least, of the enormous salary on which Lady Eleanor had insisted. But the work was seasoned with laughter and good humour, so that she greeted each new day with cheerful anticipation. Occasionally she assured herself that she was thankful that there was no dark-haired blue-eyed sea rover to disturb her peace with quizzically lifted brows or teasing grin, especially when, inevitably, she made the mistakes of inexperience.

The Gordons duly arrived and were installed in the rooms that she had so carefully prepared, and everything went smoothly. Her first experiment in ordering for a large household met with approval from Lady Eleanor, being nicely balanced between considerations of quality and economy, and the arrangements made for the nursery party were acceptable to Nurse MacNab — a triumph of the first order. Lady Eleanor was still confined to her own room, and as she and her sister were wholly absorbed in each other's society the young housekeeper found herself more fully in charge than she had anticipated, but since her first timid essays in menu planning were well received she took courage and began to enjoy her new responsibilities.

Faith was delighted with the Gordons. Though she loved her sisters dearly, twins were apt to live in their own self-contained little world, and at times she had felt a touch of loneliness. Now she was presented with a ready made family. Priscilla, only a year her junior, shared her tastes and views to a nicety, with just enough difference to add a spice to argument. Alastair and Gavin provided a liberal education to the girl who had never known the endearing and mischievous nature of small brothers, and baby Caroline was graciously pleased to accept another admirer into her circle of worshippers. Faith still slept at home, but it was about the only part of the twenty-four hours that she did spend there.

Nor was Prudence unduly bereft by the absence of her sisters, since by some odd twist of circumstance Giles Kennedy chanced to have business in the vicinity of Ash Croft with quite surprising frequency, and it would have been unneighbourly in him to have passed without calling to tell Miss Pru how her sister was sustaining the rigours of a working life.

For the past year, as he had watched her struggling bravely with tasks far too heavy for a girl, Giles had fallen ever more deeply in love with his former playmate, longing to shield her from every hardship and knowing that her pride would not permit him to do so. His position was difficult, for how could he, with so little to offer, propose marriage to a girl who would some day be a considerable heiress? Now, thanks to his cousin's offer, he was beginning to dream of an early marriage. His mother, too, was fast coming round to acceptance of Piers's suggestion; was, indeed, beginning to regard it as a most convenient disposition of all their lives. Her son should marry his Prudence, and she herself would retire to the Dower House. The Beaches would make her very comfortable and when Piers chose to come home she could play hostess for him, or if he preferred bachelor freedom she could visit Chloe or stay with her son and daughter-in-law. Perhaps by then there might even be grandchildren.

She would be sorry to part with dearest Clemency, for never before had she so enjoyed a visit from her sister, distracted as she had always been by domestic cares. But Clemency was so sweetly pretty — and an heiress, too, some far distant day — that undoubtedly she would marry well. She deserved it, thought Lady Eleanor with warm gratitude, and hoped she might marry a baronet at least.

So Piers came home to a very contented household. During his stay in Town he had arranged for a representative of Messrs. Rundell Bridge and Rundell to call upon Mr. Longden and value the jewels. He trusted that this very sensible precaution would offset the highly unusual loan terms that were to be put before that gentleman. He had been less successful in arranging his own return passage to Port Jackson, and had wasted much energy in fulminating bitterly against the stupidity of ship owners who could not foresee the splendid future that lay ahead for his adopted country. He had even contemplated investing some of his surplus wealth in the newly emergent steamship companies that would some day solve the problem of swift transport across the world. But perhaps he had better see how much his lately adopted family was like to cost him before extending his dealings too far.

That brought him back to thoughts of little Miss Longden. He wondered how she was faring in her new life. She would deal bravely, he was sure. But that life was still set in the familiar English pattern. Would her endearing quality survive transplantation, or would she sicken and droop as had the young wife of one of his friends, so that Kit had resigned a valuable holding and returned to an ill-paid job in England. It was too much to ask of any girl, he decided yet again, however much the thought of a slim little body, warm lips and candid brown eyes quickened one's pulses.

The Manor House was alive with fun and laughter when he strolled in. Great plans were afoot for a riotous Hallowe'en party, with ducking for apples and roasting of nuts and all the rites and mysteries proper to that festival, and Clemency, at the heart of it all, was too occupied with the lively brood of youngsters to pay him any attention beyond enquiring in very sedate fashion whether he would be resuming his former practice of dining with his aunt so that she might give the necessary orders. With a strong notion that the less he saw of Miss Longden the better it would be for his peace of mind, he said that in view of the irregularity of his comings and goings in the immediate future it would be better if he dined at home, but was coaxed by Faith and Priscilla into promising to do his best to attend their Hallowe'en party.

Clemency confessed to disappointment. She had rather looked forward to confounding him by her competence. A little of the savour went out of life as she accepted his decision with every appearance of indifference and turned away to separate Alastair and Gavin who were settling a fraternal argument as to which of them had created the better turnip lantern in the time honoured fashion of small boys.

Piers went home to his solitary meal, until the silence became so oppressive that he decided to drive over to Ash Croft and acquaint his neighbour with the progress he had made.

The living-room at Ash Croft was as shabby as ever, but a cheerful fire was burning on the hearth and the light of three candles illuminated the pretty picture of father and daughter at their chess table with an air of homely comfort far removed from the gloomy chill of that first visit. He apologised for the lateness of his call and begged to be allowed to watch the final stage of the battle that was being fought out. He quite expected to see Prudence permit her father to win, so was intrigued and delighted when she herself emerged the victor, and added his congratulations to her flushed enjoyment as she declared that he must have brought her luck, since Papa had won consistently over the past five nights.

"Of course he did," grinned Papa. "His coming distracted me, else I had not moved my bishop so rashly. Now, my boy, you cannot plead haste or an anxious aunt tonight, so let us crack a bottle at our leisure. It may help to sweeten the business talk that I feel is impending," and he grimaced resignedly.

Since Piers's own cellars had furnished the Chambertin that he was invited to open — no female could be trusted to handle wine properly — he hoped that this prophecy would prove true. Certainly the talk would need careful management.

Mr. Longden having approved the idea of having his wife's trinkets valued by the famous Ludgate jewellers, Piers proceeded to the far more delicate business of explaining the terms of the proposed loan.

His bankers, he said, had recommended to him a Mr. Jackson, a gentleman who combined the solid worth of a wealthy merchant with some of the eccentricity allowable in one who had travelled widely in the Orient. This client was willing to purchase the jewels outright, or, if Mr. Longden preferred it, to advance an agreed sum payable in equal proportions over the next three years against the security of the jewels, which were to be deposited with Rundell and Bridge until their full value had been paid over. They could be redeemed by their present owner at any time during this period should he find himself in a position to do so. There was one unusual proviso to the arrangement. Under no circumstances would Mr. Jackson agree to the payment of interest. It transpired that during his travels in the East he had been deeply impressed by the Moslem teaching that usury was sinful, and had set his face firmly against it in his own dealings.

Piers studied his host's attentive countenance in considerable anxiety as he came to the end of this smooth if improbable recital. He wished he had thought to invent a name less prosaic than Jackson for his imaginery eccentric. Blakeney or Devereux or something equally high sounding might have carried more conviction, but he had been thinking of his return passage and the name Jackson had come naturally into his mind. Would the tale pass muster, even with a man who admitted that he had no head for business?

"How very unusual," said Mr. Longden with deep interest. "I had no idea that these — unbelievers, I suppose we should call them — applied such lofty principles in business dealings. It seems wholly admirable and should be a lesson to all of us. I look forward to closer acquaintance with your Mr. Jackson."

Piers swallowed a mouthful of burgundy with more haste than its quality merited. "Not 'my' Mr. Jackson," he temporised smoothly. "I am not personally acquainted with him, and I rather fancy he is off on his travels again soon, but Coutts speaks highly of him and will be pleased to make all the necessary arrangements. As for the valuation representative, he is to come down in about ten days' time. I will arrange for his accommodation at the Woolpack. You will not wish to be bothered with him here. Tell me, how do you go on, now that Miss Longden has deserted you for the Manor? I hear from my aunt that she is quite invaluable, and that the boys are her devoted slaves."

Chapter Nine

THE tap room at the Woolpack offered a very cosy refuge from the dank chill of the November night, but the two customers who had arrived at dusk and appropriated the best seats in the wide chimney place did not join in the barrage of friendly chaff that rose and fell around them. Perhaps they were weary with long travel. Certainly they were both hungry and thirsty, demolishing an astounding number of the landlord's famous mutton pies and then settling down to a steady consumption of strong ale that evoked both admiration and envy from their neighbours. One or two attempted with naïve cunning to draw them out as to their business and destination, but with no success. The elder of the two answered direct questions civilly but revealed nothing of interest. When asked the state of the roads they had travelled, he said that all roads were bad and some were worse, but did not specify which. An enquiry from the smith as to any fresh news of the highwaymen who were rumoured to be active in the neighbourhood evoked a disbelieving grunt. The traveller then said sourly that he had heard tales a-plenty about such folk, but had yet to meet one.

The villagers set him down as a surly fellow and gave up in disgust. His companion spoke not at all, but maybe that was because he was of a superior station in life. He was dressed very gentlemanly in a fine mulberry cloth coat. A fine figure of a man, with powerful thighs and shoulders, and handsome enough in the dark-eyed full-blooded style. The serving maids were already discussing him in snatched whispers amid their dutiful scurryings, and had reached the conclusion that he was some young nob on the run, for they were sure he was quality make, and what would such a one be doing at the Woolpack if he were not in some sort of trouble? He reminded Dolly of the play by the travelling actors that her aunt had taken her to see. The hero had been just such a one, and it had all ended lovely, with him rescuing a lost heiress and then turning out to be a duke in disguise.

Peg cared not a fig for fine romances, her interests being of a more earthy turn. But those full red lips looked as though they could kiss a lass fit to stir the blood. She determined to set herself in his way if chance offered and flaunt her curves and dimples, and then gave chance a little assistance by being conveniently to hand when the ale in his tankard needed replenishment. Nor was her stratagem wasted, the young buck who had so taken her fancy eyeing her up and down with a knowledgeable glance that set her blushing and bridling. As she set down the new filled tankard on the bench before him, his hand came out to grasp her plump arm, and he murmured softly in her ear, "Art a tempting armful, sweetheart, with a mouth made for kisses. Shouldst not be wasting thy young sweetness serving ale to these oafs. I could show thee a better life, where thy beauty should go clad in silk."

The bold black eyes were intent on Peg's rosy face. The hand on her arm suddenly tightened its grip and jerked her towards him. She stumbled and fell against his broad chest wit a squeal of pretended protest, and shivered blissfully as he kissed her moist pink lips with casual greed. There was some laughter from the company, but the ribald comment that would normally have greeted such an incident was not forthcoming. There was something discouraging about the stranger's bearing.

He seemed to sense the stiffness in the atmosphere and released the girl with a valedictory slap on the rump and a smile, saying, with a flash of while teeth, "Shall a man be blamed for tasting such sweetness when it falls into his arms?" before turning his shoulder on the delighted Peg and fixing his gaze on the fire once more.

The older man scowled and muttered uneasily, but since no one seemed to have taken offence over the careless kiss relaxed again and supped his ale, though his keen eyes followed the flirtatious Peg with sour dislike. A proper lightskirt that one, he brooded, ready for a tumble with any lusty lad. Else Dan might have brought a bees' byke about their heads, so free as he'd handled her. Likely no harm would come of it, but there was no denying that Dan's greed for women was a weakness. Once already it had brought them close to disaster. It would have to be watched.

He spoke sternly to his fellow traveller as they made their preparations for the night in the Woolpack's homely bedchamber. His own toilet was simple, just the kicking off of his muddy boots and the removal of coat and breeches. He had washed and shaved that very morning at Dan's insistence and saw no need for further ablutions.

Dan turned a deaf ear to his dismal forebodings, stripped to the buff, and commenced a vigorous splashing in the warm water brought him by the yearning Peg, after which he checked the priming of a serviceable looking pistol and tucked it under his pillow.

Harry eyed the weapon with disfavour. "And that's another thing. You're a sight too handy with that pop of yours. Why did you have to go shooting that poor devil Thomson when he went for you? What's more I don't blame him. Any man as was a man would have tried to do for you. That brat of his that you forced was no more than eight years old, and how you can fancy such chicken meat is more than I can see. But no matter for that. What I says and what I sticks by is that there was no need to go shooting him. What's more it's made Alverstock too hot to hold us."

Dan yawned widely, showing his magnificent teeth, and stretched powerful arms luxuriously. "You're a fool, Harry. Thomson had to die. He'd have betrayed us as fast as he could get to the nearest roundhouse. And don't tell me he was in the business as deep as any of us. Of course he was — but he'd not have cared for that so long as he could have made sure that I'd swing along of him."

"Then why couldn't you let his miserable skinny brat alone?"

A smile that was wholly evil curved the mouth that had set Peg's heart a-flutter. "Because I like 'em little and frightened, Harry boy," he said softly. "When they struggle and weep and beg for mercy, I like it all the more. That silly wench below stairs with her mouth all a-slobber, there's plenty of her sort. I take 'em, see, if I'm in the mood, for a gentleman should always oblige a lady, but there's little pleasure in it. No. It's chicken meat for me, Harry, as you so aptly phrased it. I've a dainty palate. Small and young and terrified."

Harry looked at him curiously. Over the months of their association he had come to accept most of Dan's peculiarities. Some of them — his ability to ape the gentleman for instance — were very useful. His refusal to use cant or foul language, his preoccupation with his appearance, above all the frequency with which he washed, had even made Harry think him a bit of a fop. He knew better now. The man was rock hard. He would rob, disable, murder, quite unmoved by the agonies of his victims, and his cool nerve and inventive mind had lifted the pair of them out of many a tight corner. His only known weakness was his appetite for women, but since there were plenty of willing fools eager to succumb to his handsome face and practised love making, Harry saw no harm in his leader satisfying the natural lusts of a virile man so long as such preoccupations did not distract him from business.

But this was something different again; something twisted and rotten. Harry, who regarded violence and murder as practical necessities in the search for gain, was suddenly sickened by this gloating over the pain and terror of a puny girl child. Furtively, behind his back, he made the age old sign against evil, learned from his mother in the days of his innocence. Then he shrugged off his revulsion and changed the subject.

"Where's the booberkin?" he demanded, as Dan stretched himself on the bed and blew out the candle.

"With the horses at the Wyke barn," grunted Dan, digging himself into a more comfortable position. "He's not due here till tomorrow forenoon. The grey was to be tricked out as a piebald and Rufus becomes a black. No one'll recognise that pair when Overing's done with them. He's most as good as he claimed to be. Let alone his handiness with the clippers and dye-pot, he can even manage Lucifer."

"I don't trust him," growled Harry jealously. "First time he sees the claret flow in earnest he'll be struck all of a heap. Lily livered for all his big talk."

Dan yawned again. "It's no matter. He knows naught to harm us. If he does become a nuisance —" He allowed the sentence to trail off into the darkness. "Meanwhile we bide quietly here. I've a fancy to size up the lay of the land before we go to work."

"That's well enough," said Harry, "but slumming kens is what I don't hold with. I'd as lief put my head in a trap. I like the open road and a good beast between my knees."

"You'll have a rope round your neck, never mind your head in a trap, if you use that thieves' cant here," snapped Dan. "We're two decent sober fellows on the look out for some promising young stock, such as'll make good sound hunters when they've filled out a bit, and don't you forget it. Gives us a good reason for looking around, and by the time we're ready to do the job these dumb cattle'll have got so used to seeing us about they'll pay no heed to our comings and goings. I'll admit I'd like a bit more information myself, but a man must make do with what he can get, and all that Barney could tell us was that the sparkle merchant was booked on next Friday's coach. All we've to do is stick to his track. Like as not he'll take the stuff back with him and it should be a simple enough job to relieve him of his burden. But whether it falls out that way, or whether we have to break into the old gager's house, we're having those sparklers, or my name's not Dan Pelly."

"And the lad knows nothing?"

"D'you take me for a fool? He thinks we're out to stop a few chaises, hold up the Mail, maybe, and is all set to be a romantical daredevil — when his teeth stop shattering with fright. *He's* no use to us, 'cept for tending the nags. A deal of flash talk, but no bottom."

Since this was precisely Harry's own opinion of young Overing's capabilities, he said no more, and presently his peaceful snores indicated that he had abandoned further mental effort for the time being.

Chapter Ten

FAITH came dancing into the still-room where Clemency, with a very housewifely air, was tying up pots of crabapple jelly, holding each to the light to ensure that no trace of murky brown marred its rosy perfection.

"Darling, darling Clee," she bubbled. "The most wonderful thing. Please say I may go. Papa will agree if you do!"

"Go where, rattlepate?"

"To London," breathed Faith ecstatically. "With the Gordons. Mrs. Gordon thinks I would be a suitable friend and companion for Priscilla, and even Nurse MacNab says that I have been a help with the boys. Of course I wouldn't get a salary like you, but Papa would be spared the cost of my keep. Lady Eleanor approves the scheme and says it is time I learned how I should go on in Society. And oh, Clee! On the way we are to stay in York for a sennight with some cousins, and Mrs. Gordon has promised she will take Priscilla and me to the play. We are too young for the Assemblies she says, but it will be perfectly proper for us to go to the play if it is a respectable one. Cilia says she will lend me her brown sarsenet which is too tight for her, and with my gold locket and chain I shall look quite the thing. Please, please, dearest of sisters — say that I may go!"

Clemency could not help feeling the bite of envy. If only she, too, were off on her travels into the wider world that beckoned so alluringly! York and London might sound humdrum compared with her girlish dreams of travels that should put even Lady Hester Stanhope to shame, but she had never seen either city, and the thought of the journeying and the fresh sights to be seen filled her heart with longing.

She set down the last pot of jelly with a steady hand and smiled at her glowing little sister. "I'm sure Papa will agree," she said gently. "It is just what he would wish for you. But we shall have to bustle about to have you ready in time. You *must* have one or two new gowns. And you will need some money in your pocket. You cannot be dependent on the Gordons for every penny."

The child deserved the treat. Her sunny nature and equable temper had endeared her to the whole family, else the generous offer had never been made. But Faith's going would also mark the end of her own usefulness. Lady Eleanor would be eager to resume her own responsibilities once her relatives were gone. But repining would do no good, and no doubt this was all part of being independent. One found a post which suited like a glove, and then had to move on when no longer needed. Resolutely she bent her mind to the problem of equipping Faith decently for a visit of unspecified duration.

There was scant time for brooding during the few remaining days of the Gordons' stay. Clemency found herself occupied far into the night with sewing and packing, so that it was almost with relief that she stood beside Lady Eleanor waving farewell as the coach rolled away down the avenue. As the second coach carrying the luggage and Nurse with the boys and baby Caroline passed out of sight at the end of the road, she drew a deep sigh and turned to Lady Eleanor with a rather tremulous smile.

"That's right, my dear," said the elder lady encouragingly. Let her go without foolish tears. They would only dim her happiness, and you know very well that it is great good fortune that Chloe should have taken such a fancy to her. She will look after her as your mother would have done. You need have no fears for your sister when she is in the care of *mine*." And laughing a little at this mild pleasantry, she drew Clemency back into the house, saying kindly, "Now we shall have a comfortable coze together before we set about the task of putting all to rights again."

With the house so full Lady Eleanor had not had the opportunity of confidential talk with her nephew. She wondered if he had been further inspired with regard to his protégée's future. She had never before known him to show such interest in any female. It was a pity that his admiration for the girl's brave spirit was not likely to lead to a warmer concern, but he had shown no sign of trying to fix his interest with her. Perhaps he was still resolved that marriage was not for him. Briskly she dismissed idle speculation and spoke of the furbishing up of the guest rooms that she had in mind for the next few days. In carrying out this task, Clemency's hands and feet were certainly kept busy, but her mind was all too frequently free to ponder a desolate future.

She felt the lonelier because it was becoming increasingly apparent that the close link with her twin was a thing of the past. Each time that she went home she found Pru more lovely and more absent minded. Good food was rounding out the hollows in cheeks and throat, and happiness had added a bewitching bloom. Her interest in her sister's affairs was at best perfunctory. Admitted that Clemency's talk was of domestic detail and rather dull, yet it was new and depressing to find her twin too self-absorbed to enter into her small triumphs and comic mishaps. It seemed that both her sisters were launched into the world. Horizons were widening for Faith, and though there was as yet no formal betrothal between Pru and Giles it was abundantly clear that romance was in the air. Clemency rejoiced sincerely in her sister's good fortune, but inevitably it pointed the contrast with her own. She loved Papa dearly, but the thought of spending all the days of her youth at Ash Croft in virtual seclusion and bereft even of her sisters' company did nothing to lift her spirits. Driving Jenny back to the Manor she even shed a few slow tears of self-pity. Then, deeply ashamed of such weakness, hurried up to her room to remove the tear stains and change her dress for dinner.

She came down to the hall a little later expecting to find Lady Eleanor alone, for Giles had gone off to York to escort his aunt on the first stage of her journey and was not expected back for another day or so. It was surprising, therefore, to see a pair of long and undoubtedly masculine legs protruding from the chair in which their owner was indolently disposed, a wineglass in one hand, the other gesturing freely in illustration of some inaudible tale.

It seemed that she had only to set eyes on Captain Kennedy to feel a sense of irritation. Her housekeeping was not so inadequate that it would not stretch to an extra appetite, or, indeed, to several, yet her first thought was that he might at least have told them that he would be coming to dinner. Then she realised that the hand holding the wineglass was bandaged, and anxiety drove out annoyance as she hurried down the last three steps and came towards the fire.

Lady Eleanor glanced up with a concerned expression as Piers rose to make his bow.

"Do sit down," she begged him. "Clemency will surely excuse you. For all you make so light of it, you must have lost a deal of blood, and if I had my way you'd be in bed. For sure you should not be drinking wine. Enough to set you in a high fever."

Her graceless nephew grinned tolerantly over her fussing. "You'll have Miss Longden thinking me at death's door," he said lazily. "Which I assure you, dearest of aunts, I am not. 'Tis only in my temper and my pride that I am sorely wounded. To think that I should be taken in by such a childish stratagem!"

"But surely any true gentleman would have stopped to help a female in distress," said his aunt indignantly.

Piers laughed. "Any gentleman who was sufficiently wide awake would have seen that this female stood in sore need of a shave!" retorted. "As well as standing some six feet tall. But at least I winged the impudent rascal before he shot the gun out of my hand." He looked ruefully at his bandaged fingers. "It's a damnable nuisance to be so incommoded just now when I have so much writing to do. My apologies, ladies, for my forceful language. Set it down to my recent discomfiture."

Had Piers known that his late adversary was enduring a vicious tongue lashing from his wrathful associate in that snug bedchamber at the Woolpack, he might have been a little comforted.

"Thrice born idiot and numskull," snarled Pelly, his face twisted with venom, "I told you to bide quiet, didn't I? But no. You must go skylarking about with young Overing. And all for some country lout with scarce a six-pence to jingle in his pockets. I'm *glad* he put a bullet through you. A pity his aim was no better." He pulled the bandage tight over the rough and ready pad. "It's naught but a graze, and you'll keep your great mouth shut about it, d'you hear?"

Harry winced at the rough handling. "I meant no harm," he muttered sullenly. "The lad said he knew the cull — leastways he recognised the turnout — and reckoned he was a well breeched 'un. 'Twould have worked all right if he hadn't been so quick with his barker. Lucky I shot it out of his hand. I reckoned a few guineas would come in handy like, with us wasting the ready in high living and waiting about."

"So for a few paltry guineas you'd risk a fortune in jewels. Let one whisper of suspicion fall on us, and the game's up. You fool, Harry. I'm minded to send you back to Barney and tell him I'll manage best alone."

The words were mild. But Harry's face paled to a sickly green and his hard-bitten features seemed to crumple and disintegrate at what amounted, he knew, to a threat of execution. "I'll not meddle no more, Dan," he pleaded hoarsely. "And who's to be a whit the wiser for today's ploy? Will stayed under cover, and the cove we stopped'll never recognise me again, seeing I was wearing woman's gear. All's bowman, Dan."

"Is it, indeed?" The voice was still silkily dangerous. "It's your good fortune, Harry boy, that the fellow from Rundell and Bridge comes in tomorrow on the night Mail. Booked in for three days, my lovely Peg tells me. So I *may* — I just *may* — need you. But you'll leave him alone, Harry.

No trying to be clever and drawing him into conversation. You're ill equipped for a task that needs brains. *You* can take a ride in the direction of this Ash Croft place, and look it over. Study the — er — jiggers and glazes, I believe you would call them, in your fancy cant — and find out how the place is staffed, just in case we have to break in."

"How the devil am I to find that out?" demanded Harry sullenly, recovered now from his fright and resenting the aspersion on his mental powers. "Do I ring the bell and ask how many footmen they keep?"

"You do indeed ring the bell," explained his mentor with grim patience. "But you ask for direction to a place called the Manor, where there's some squireling that breeds hunters and hacks, so our worthy landlord informs me. If you cannot judge the strength of the opposition by the style of the place, and whether it is a liveried man who opens the door rather than some maid servant, then you had best retire to the Metropolis and exercise your talents in picking pockets."

"You and your breaketeeth words," muttered Harry grumpily; and then, more cheerfully, "If I'm to make no mention of this —" he moved his wounded arm and grimaced at its soreness — "then I'm for a heavy wet and a bite to eat. Though I *could* have said that I'd been in a brush with these highwaymen they're always on about." He grinned at this happy thought, and went on, "Quite the hero I'd have been. All the company buying me drinks, like as not." Then, at the ominous tightening of Dan's lips, "Only funning, Dan, only funning. Just as you say. I'll make no mention of it. I'll sit mum as a mouse when the cat's at the hole," and removed himself thankfully from that dangerous proximity to go downstairs in search of refreshment.

Lady Eleanor and Clemency had also been eager to discuss every detail of so shocking an attempt at a hold-up in broad daylight, and Piers had succeeded, to his great content, in making it sound more comical than frightening. It was as they were moving towards the dining-room — Piers having insisted that a beefsteak, lightly grilled, would be much more effective in building up his strength than any invalid messes (and also more to his taste) — that Clemency asked, "Was there only the one man concerned? The one who stopped your curricle? He must have had a horse concealed somewhere. Where exactly did he stop you?"

"I did see — or imagine — a second man lurking among the trees," admitted Piers. "But it was all over so quickly. The horses were alarmed by the shooting and I had some ado to get them under control again. By that time my assailant had vanished, and it seemed foolish to go searching the coppice for traces of lurkers, especially as I was dripping blood all over my best breeches."

Lady Eleanor shuddered, but Clemency persisted in her enquiries as to the exact location of the attack.

"Coming up Nab Hill," said Piers. "It's steepish, and I was letting the horses take it easily. They'd had a pretty gruelling day. There's a derelict cottage stands back from the road and a screen of trees about it. That's where I thought I saw the other fellow."

"I know the place you mean," nodded his aunt. "There's a horrid tale about that cottage. It used to be a respectable farm holding, but one morning the farmer's wife was found hanged in the barn, and her husband was never seen again. No one would live there after that. It's just the sort of place that one can imagine thieves and highwaymen using as a shelter. But pray let us discuss some pleasanter topic, for this one is like to give us poor females the nightmare!"

Piers obligingly recounted the less spectacular events of his day. Both ladies were able to take an interest in his account of the mill that he had visited, even though its products were designed mainly for masculine wear.

"And to think that Giles may actually wear a broadcloth or a superfine that came originally from your flocks!" marvelled Lady Eleanor. "It is quite fascinating. Have you many more such visits to make?"

Piers shrugged ruefully. "Several more than I intended, thanks to my friend on Nab Hill. It's a cursed nuisance, since it takes up so much more time, but I can still handle a team, even if I can't write letters."

Clemency looked across at Lady Eleanor. "Could I not write Captain Kennedy's letters for him?" she asked diffidently. "I am thought to write a good plain hand, and I *can* spell. Would not that be adequate to your needs, Sir? You have only to tell me what you wish said. That is if Lady Eleanor can spare me, of course."

"An excellent scheme, my dear," approved that lady. "Do you not agree, Piers?"

Piers was decidedly averse to the idea of females having anything to do with business, believing that they had neither method nor discretion, and in this particular case it was quite essential that Mistress Clemency should not be placed in a position where she might inadvertently discover the truth about certain of his recent dealings. But he was sorely tempted. For a whole fortnight he had stuck grimly to his resolution to avoid the girl, and in the press of business it had not been too difficult. He felt that he had earned some small reward for such virtuous conduct — and here it was, being tossed into his lap.

"I fear you would find it very dull, Miss Longden," he demurred.

"That I certainly should not," she denied eagerly. "I make no doubt that to you it is all perfectly commonplace, but to me it is exciting, even romantic, that the stuff of my gown —" she fingered its amber folds lovingly — "should come from that strange, wonderful land which Captain Flinders explored. I could only wish it were woven into a magic carpet that might transport me across the world to see for myself. But you are laughing at me" — and indeed he was smiling appreciatively at the eager glowing face — "so I will say only that I would be both pleased and proud if I might help, even in so small a way, in your enterprise."

"Then if Aunt Eleanor will consent to lend you to me for two or three hours each morning, I will accept your offer most gratefully."

"Where will you choose to work, Piers?" asked Lady Eleanor. "The estate office? It is unused while Giles is away."

"If Miss Longden does not object to it, I would prefer to work in my own library, where all the materials and papers are ready to hand. It scarcely seems worth the pains of transporting them all up here for a matter of two or three days."

"And Mrs. Beach will be chaperone sufficient," nodded Lady Eleanor equably.

A swift side glance at his new secretary revealed a countenance slightly flushed and eyes demurely downcast, reasonable evidence that Miss Longden was recalling an occasion when that chaperonage had certainly not sufficed. What did she really feel about that occasion, wondered Piers. Her manner towards him had varied from icy reserve to impertinent teasing and simple friendliness, but she had never betrayed any sign that she found him attractive as a man. Yet when he had held her in his arms he had sensed the promise of a response as warm and sweet as a man could desire. He tried to banish the memory of that forbidden sweetness, and said with grave courtesy, "Then shall we say at ten tomorrow morning? That would allow time to have the letters sent off by the evening mail. I will not task you too heavily the first day, for you will find the terms of the trade strange and new, however good your spelling!"

Chapter Eleven

CLEMENCY presented herself for duty punctually at ten o'clock, outwardly composed save for such a minor detail as shaking, ice cold fingers, a weakness which she covered by keeping them tightly gripped on the pen case which she was carrying as a badge of office. She had spent considerable time in the night watches in regretting her impulsive offer, which had suddenly loomed up as forward and unmaidenly, forcing her society on one who, of late, had shown no wish to seek it. Common sense had revived a little in the clear light of day. Surely Captain Kennedy would see her suggestion as a natural and friendly one, and read no more into it than that. Nevertheless her manner was so hesitant that Piers felt she might turn and run if he made an injudicious move or remark. With just that air of bright but timid fascination must Red Riding Hood have eyed the wolf.

Greetings exchanged and the progress of the injured fingers casually dismissed, he explained the arrangement of the cases of samples. There seemed to be a great many of them, and Piers spent some time in describing the different qualities, uses and prices of lambs' wool, hogg wool, combing, short staple and several more until his pupil forgot her shyness and assailed him with questions which he answered very patiently until she became guiltily aware of the passage of time and broke off in mid sentence to say, "Oh, dear! The letters!"

He assured her that the time had not been wasted since she would need to recognise the samples and know where to find them. Then he set a chair for her at the desk and began to pull open drawers and spread copies of letters before her until the desk began to assume the same cluttered appearance that it had worn when Clemency first set eyes upon it. He showed her the sort of letter that was required this morning and furnished her with a list of the manufacturers to whom it should be addressed. It seemed simple enough, and she settled to the task with modest confidence.

She very soon discovered, however, that concentrating on accuracy and penmanship with someone else in the room was not so easy as she had thought. Piers had gone back to the cabinet which held the samples and seemed wholly engrossed in setting it in order, clumsily marking numbers on some of the paper folders with his left hand. Though his movements were quiet she found herself continually glancing in his direction, interrupting her work and losing her place. Presently she had to scratch out a word that she had written twice. She took a fresh sheet of paper and began again, determined that the document should be as perfect as she could make it. Her face grew hot and her lips were so tightly folded together that she looked quite fierce. Piers, studying her unobtrusively, and sensitively aware of her difficulty, found the picture both comical and touchingly young. One foot was twisted round the leg of the chair which was a little too high for her, her hair was already slightly ruffled, and there was a spatter of ink across one cheek. Presently he heard a big sigh of relief as she finished the first letter.

He strolled across to glance at it and she waited anxiously for his verdict. "That's very good," he pronounced judicially. "Perfectly clear and neatly set out. I waited in case you met with any difficulty, but you obviously understand exactly what is needed, so perhaps you would prefer to be left alone."

The thankful tone in which she promptly cried out, "Oh! Yes, please. I wish you will go at once!" tickled him enormously. He looked down at her, a wicked gleam in the blue eyes, and said sadly, "It seems I played the ogre better than I dreamed at our first meeting, since you are so anxious to be rid of me."

Clemency blushed furiously, realising the enormity of her words, and hurried into incoherent apology. He found her confusion quite adorable, and permitted her to stumble among penitent half sentences as she tried to explain her true meaning, then laughed down at her, but gently, and bade her pluck up heart. "For indeed I was but teasing, knowing perfectly well how much I, too, dislike having anyone in the room when I am writing letters."

She smiled back at him gratefully, and so confidingly that the moment at last seemed opportune for him to repair a much regretted omission. "Since I have at last dared to recall to your memory the — er — unusual circumstances of our first meeting, may I know if you can find it in your heart to forgive my shocking behaviour on that occasion? I was on the verge of humble apology when Giles walked in on us, and having let that opportunity slip by, it seemed prudent to allow the memory of your injuries to fade a little before suing for pardon."

He sounded so very humble, so truly sorry, that she risked a glance at him. His mouth was certainly composed in lines of serious appeal but his eyes were full of mischief and set in laughter creases, so that she put her pretty little nose in the air and said tartly, "Your looks belie you, Sir. You do not seem to me to stand in such sore need of my forgiveness!" and picked up her pen with a strange little ache at her heart for some cause that she could not quite define.

His hand came down to catch hers, his injured hand, so that she could not pull away as sharply as she would have wished for fear of hurting him. "If you please, Sir," she said coldly, glancing pointedly at that masterful hand. "Pray permit me to resume my task. The morning is already far spent."

"You shall do so, my child, as soon as we have settled this vastly more important matter," he replied, voice and countenance now wholly serious. "I am utterly sincere in seeking your forgiveness for the shock and fear that I deliberately inflicted upon you," he said quietly, his eyes holding hers with a determination that she should accept his word. "If I could erase them from your memory, I would most thankfully do so. You will believe me?"

With that intense blue gaze fixed upon hers, she could only nod dumbly. She did indeed believe him. If ever a man meant what he said, this one did.

The stern lines about his mouth relaxed. Gently he raised her hand in his and brushed it lightly with his lips. "The kiss of peace," he explained gravely as he released her fingers. "And I am fully forgiven?"

"Why, of course, Sir," dimpled a suddenly happier Clemency, and added, with doubtful truth, "You make too much ado. I had almost forgot."

His lips quivered irrepressibly, and his deep soft chuckle startled her, so that she stepped back a pace. "You do well to retreat on that remark," he said severely. "Of all the shocking bouncers! You have *not* forgotten, any more than I have. You will recall that I did not express any regret for kissing you the second time? How could I, when the experience was so wholly delightful? You are a very tempting morsel for an ogre to gobble up, my girl, and I deeply regret that some dim memory of the proper behaviour in which I was bred forces me to hold you sacrosanct while you are in my service. It is as much for my own sake as for yours that I am about to remove myself. There is great good sense in fleeing the temptation that one is vowed to resist." With which astonishing speech he bowed to her with some ceremony and walked cut of the room.

Miss Longden did not at once resume her secretarial labours. There was food for much thought in that brief exchange, and for even more delicious speculation. There was a mirror set into the front of the cabinet that held the wool samples. She got up and walked over to it. For a girl who had never in her life received a compliment from a man, it was intoxicating to be told that she offered a temptation difficult to resist. She studied her reflection earnestly, half expecting to notice some new born charm. Alas! She looked just as usual — rather worse than usual, with ink on her face. If only her hair was a fashionable colour instead of just golden brown, or curled naturally as Faith's did, instead of hanging silken straight. She had long abandoned the attempt at a smart style and contented herself with braiding it and piling it on top of her head in the hope that it would at least make her look taller. It never occurred to her that a man might dream of loosening the sweet scented braids, of drawing the silky stuff through his fingers and burying his face in its brown-gold depths.

She turned her back on the mirror's impartiality and crossed to the hearth to replenish the crumbling fire with fresh logs, lingering to gaze at the little running flames in blissful reverie. He had spoken truth when he vowed that she had not forgotten, though indeed she had made a valiant endeavour to put him out of her mind. Now, deliberately, she recalled how it had felt to be held close in his arms and kissed; and this time without the fear of the unknown that had filled her. It seemed as though the little flames that were licking over the logs had crept into her own veins, bringing a delicious sensuous warmth. A smile, half eager, half mischievous, dimpled her cheek, and she whispered softly to the glowing heart of the fire, "How if temptation prove too strong for his notions of propriety?"

And then, quite shocked to hear such an improper possibility suggested, even in a whisper, she sprang up and returned to her place at the desk, though still a long period of pen nibbling ensued before, with a deep sigh, she dipped the maltreated implement into the ink and began to write. Nor did her powers of concentration appear to benefit from her solitary state, for there were long pauses between the bursts of industrious application. She was quite horrified when Beach came into the room to ask if she would take a nuncheon or if she would be returning to the Manor.

"Pray tell Mrs. Beach how sorry I am to put her to so much trouble. If I could have a cup of coffee and some bread and butter, it will be quite sufficient. Then I can finish the letters in time for the evening mail, as Captain Kennedy wished."

Mrs. Beach, not averse to showing that stuck up Betsy a trick or two, very properly ignored this foolish request. Clemency was shortly invited to the parlour, where, in addition to cold meat and fruit, a dish of buttered eggs, some broiled pigeons and a dish of new baked cheese curd cakes had been set out for her delectation, while Beach, promising that she should have her coffee later, brought her a glass of 'the master's best Madeira' which he assured her wouldn't hurt her a mite. She sipped it cautiously, decided that it did not go with buttered eggs but might not taste too bad with cheese cakes, and proceeded to make an excellent meal, thereby earning Mrs. Beach's wholehearted commendation.

"That's a sensible well brought up young lady," she informed her spouse. "One that knows good food when she sees it and eats hearty but not greedy," this last as her eye fell on the untouched pigeons. Clemency had not been able to bring herself to taste those pathetic looking morsels. They would do very nicely for her husband's supper, decided Mrs. Beach, baked up in a pastry case.

Perhaps the meal — or the Madeira — exercised a soothing effect on the emotions, for work proceeded quite steadily thereafter, with only one brief interlude spent in poring over the copy letter, not for its content which she now had by heart, but for a closer study of the firm square script in which it was written. She had almost finished when she heard sounds of arrival. There was the clatter of hard driven horses, followed swiftly by the sound of the front door-bell set ringing by a peremptory hand. There was scarce time to wonder who had come visiting in such urgency when the library door was flung open and Faith stood upon the threshold with Giles at her shoulder, a Faith with countenance so changed from the merry rosy face to which Clemency had waved farewell that she sprang to her feet, knocking over the heavy chair in her dismay as she ran to her sister. Eyes huge and dark in a white strained face, Faith moistened dry lips with her tongue, swallowed convulsively and gulped out, "I've found Mama!" and burst into hysterical weeping as she cast herself into Clemency's arms.

Chapter Twelve

"NOTHING would do but that she must come herself and at once," explained Giles. "She would have set out last night if my aunt would have permitted it. As it is we started before daylight, and she has eaten nothing all day. What with the shock and the distress of finding your mother in such a sorry way, it is little wonder that she is in this state. Plucky little soul really, and sensible too. Said at once it was you must hear the news first and would know how best to break it to your father. Mama says she had best stay with us tonight, and I'm to take you both back to her at once."

Most of this discourse made but little impression on Clemency's dazed mind. She was more concerned with trying to soothe Faith. The wild sobbing gradually subsided and presently the child was sitting up, mopping her tearstained cheeks with Giles's handkerchief, and trying to tell her story. But the tale was so disjointed, so broken by hiccupping sobs, that Clemency begged her to wait until she was more composed and asked Giles if he would desire Mrs. Beach to make some tea.

This drunk, Faith was steadier and able to tell her tale more coherently, her voice and manner growing more sensible and collected as she went on.

On the previous evening Mrs. Gordon had fulfilled her promise of taking the two girls to the theatre. It had been afterwards, as they were emerging from Lop Lane and walking towards Museum Street where the carriage was to meet them that Faith, pausing to re-tie a loosened sandal string, had straightened up almost under the noses of two women who were walking in the opposite direction. Her attention was caught by the fact that one of them was so heavily veiled that it was impossible to discern her features. It was then that a casual glance at the lady's attendant brought instant recognition.

"Elsie!" Faith had said sharply, not even realising that she had spoken aloud.

Second thoughts might have caused her to doubt her identification of her mother's maid. After all it was four years since she had seen the woman.

But on hearing her name spoken she had halted, turned, and cried out, "Miss Faith!"

By this time the rest of the party had turned back to see what was delaying the girls, and if Elsie had wished to deny the mutual recognition and make her escape — as her subsequent behaviour suggested — it was too late. Mrs. Gordon, gathering that the stranger might be able to give news of Faith's mother, said that they could not discuss so intimate a matter in the public street and had better move on towards the waiting carriage. Elsie had accompanied them most unwillingly, protesting that she had thought the young lady said "Effie". Faith had said, "But you knew me, too. You called me Miss Faith," but Elsie instantly denied this, insisting that all she had said was that it was a *mistake*, and vowing that she had never seen the young lady before.

At this point they had reached the waiting carriage, and it was here that the veiled lady took a hand in resolving the matter. In the general excitement no one had particularly noticed that she had quietly accompanied them, and she had taken no part in the argument that rose and fell about her. But now she spoke, pronouncing happily in clear and cultured tones, "Oh! A carriage! How delightful, Elsie. It is so long since I have ridden in a carriage."

At the first words in that dear familiar voice Faith had sprung forward, her face filled with a wild incredulous joy. But it was abundantly clear, even without the restraining hand of the now proven Elsie, that something was very wrong. There was no mutual recognition here.

"Don't, Miss," muttered Elsie, half sullen, half supplicating. "She doesn't know you. She doesn't know anybody. She's forgotten who she is, and you'll only upset her."

Here Giles had suggested that they had better all get into the carriage and go home, where they could sort things out in decent privacy. One or two people were already loitering in their vicinity with obvious interest, and only the fact that it had begun to rain had prevented the gathering of a crowd.

It was not very far to the house in Coney Street where they were staying. Upon arrival, Mrs. Gordon explained matters to her cousin and secured the privacy of a small saloon on the first floor to which Elsie and her veiled companion were escorted. It was then that Faith could almost have wished herself back at Ash Croft, with no wonderful discovery made, for that well remembered voice was saying pleasantly, "What a pretty apartment! That is quite the most charming Meissen figure I have seen in an age. A fruit seller, is she not?" and slender hands were removing the veil to show Faith her mother's face.

It seemed impossible that she would not hold out welcoming arms, so unchanged did she seem from that dear Mama who had so often greeted a homecoming schoolgirl with a loving hug. Then she turned to look for Elsie, and Faith's sharp gasp of shock and horror was blessedly lost in the remarks she was addressing in an undervoice to her maid. Giles and Mrs. Gordon heard the pathetic lost note in the sweet voice as she murmured, "I'm so sorry, Elsie. I'm afraid I've forgotten again. Are we staying here tonight?" They could not guess at the shattering effect on Elsie when that voice continued, "Is Mr. Longden to join me here?" Mrs. Gordon, seeing the woman's terrified gaze, moved forward and suggested gently that perhaps Mrs. Longden would like to rest awhile, and then when the enquiry for her husband was repeated, improvised rapidly to explain that Mr. Longden had been delayed but would be joining them as soon as possible.

"Then if you will forgive me, I think I *will* retire to my room," said Mrs. Longden with that sweet vague smile. "I cannot think why it is, but I have the headache a little. Such shocking behaviour in a guest, but I know you will understand," and she drifted towards the door.

"*My* room," Mrs. Gordon had almost hissed at the startled Giles, and then with an imperative nod to Elsie, "See that she has all she needs, and do not leave her until she is asleep. My nephew will show you."

During the long interval that followed Faith gave way to a flood of tears. "Her face," she sobbed into Mrs. Gordon's lap. "Her poor lovely face!"

For the lifting of the veil had shown the left side of Mrs. Longden's face to be seamed and scarred from brow to chin in hideous fashion, her hair bleached white, and her appearance all the more shocking because, viewed from the other side, she was still a very lovely woman.

Mrs. Gordon wisely allowed the child to sob out her grief with no more attempt at comfort than a few gentle pats and crooning noises such as she used in soothing her children's nursery sorrows. When she judged that the storm was abating a little she said firmly, "Now, my dear, you have wept enough. There is much cause for rejoicing, and much to be done. Nor need you give up hope that in God's good time your mother's mental faculties may be restored. She has evidently been involved in some dreadful accident, and though the scarring of her face is very sad, the loss of her memory was far worse. If I understood the matter aright, she did not even know who she was. Tonight you heard her recall her husband's name. Though she did not recognise *you*, it may well have been your presence that revived the springs of memory. We must move slowly and carefully, but I see no reason for such despair as you are indulging."

Faith dried her eyes obediently. Mrs. Gordon pulled the bell and desired the maid who answered it to bring a glass of hot milk. Faith was positive she couldn't swallow anything, but good manners and gratitude alike insisted that she try, and having managed a few sips she felt a good deal better, and had drunk more than half of it before Giles came back with a very subdued Elsie.

Elsie Scales had a good deal of explaining to do, thought Mrs. Gordon. But she was a humane woman, and the sight of the servant's worn and tragic face moved her to kindness. She bade Giles set a chair for her, and offered refreshment, but Elsie, imprisoned in a world of horror of her own creating, shook her head and waited dumbly for the inquisition to begin.

Since Faith was the only one of them who knew the details of her mother's disappearance, it fell to her to question the poor soul. And her frank questions, her absorbed interest, and her patent sympathy with Elsie's sufferings, helped the girl to forget her own share in the responsibility for the tragedy, and brought the tale tumbling out in a breathless flood of narrative that ended in tears and desolation.

For Elsie it had been heartbreak. Fresh from the country and utterly ignorant of the ways of the world, she had fallen into converse with a chance met stranger at an inn where they had stopped for refreshment and a change of horses on their way south. There had been some small delay, so that the acquaintance had time to ripen, and when the young man turned up in Richmond and put himself to the pains of waylaying her when she went on errands for her mistress, she had been flattered and excited and soon began to fancy herself in love.

The man was handsome and smooth-spoken, and his obvious interest in Elsie's small affairs persuaded her that his intentions were serious. She began to dream of wedding bells, with never the least inkling that she was being skilfully drawn out as to the financial standing of her employer. On this head, regrettably, she exaggerated a little. It was understandable. Her Daniel was such a smart young fellow, so well versed in all matters of 'ton'. She feared that he might look down on her rustic simplicity. So comfortable Ash Croft became a palatial residence, the family's standing in the County was second to none, and Mrs. Longden's fortune and valuable jewellery grew, on Elsie's lips, to fabulous proportions.

With much time on her hands, and a kindly mistress who was pleased that her maid, too, should enjoy the holiday, there was no hindrance to the growing intimacy between the two. Daniel seemed to be comfortably circumstanced and mentioned that he was thinking of setting up his own livery stable. He took Elsie driving in a very respectable carriage that he had just purchased. So when her mistress decided, suddenly, that she could not endure a longer separation from husband and home, it was only natural that Elsie should suggest that her new friend should be employed to take them into Richmond to make enquiries at the Star and Garter about hiring a chaise for the journey back to Yorkshire.

Mrs. Longden had already heard a good deal about Elsie's admirer. Had she not been so preoccupied with her own problems she would have sought an opportunity before this to look the young man over. Now that the opportunity presented itself so conveniently she was pleased to take advantage of it. A delighted Elsie was despatched to ask her beau to bring his vehicle round to the house in an hour's time.

Repairing to the modest hostelry which he had favoured with his patronage, Elsie found the young man, for the first time since they had met, a little less than smooth, a little less ready to acquiesce smilingly in all her wishes. He looked hot and harassed, and there was mud on his clothes. This dishevelled appearance was soon explained. He had been out riding, and upon his return had received news of the sudden death of a gentleman — no, not a relative or close friend, just one with whom he had business dealings, but whose death could cause complications. Daniel must ride to London at once to set matters in train for an orderly solution.

Elsie was sadly downcast. "Could you not spare the time to take Mistress and me into Richmond first?" she pleaded. "It is not so very far out of your way — and we could hire a chaise to bring us back."

He hesitated briefly, then with a flash of white teeth smiled at the adoring wench and conceded her wish. "Since you desire it so much, my dear," he bowed.

Home she ran to say that all was arranged, and then in eager haste to change into her prettiest gown.

Daniel Pelly, who had shot and killed a man that morning in a mismanaged hold-up on Barnes Common, and who feared that the authorities were already on his track, shrugged, and returned to his hurried packing. So wealthy a woman as Mrs. Longden would doubtless carry a well filled purse. It was a pity that she was unlikely to be wearing much jewellery at this time of day, but the guineas would be useful and he might as well get his hands on them since his schemes were now set all awry by this morning's mishap.

With modest self-possession he bore his presentation to Mrs. Longden who was pleasantly impressed by his respectful manners and polite address. Willingly she agreed to being driven into town by a slightly devious route which would, he promised, present some charming views. There was no particular reason for haste, though it was a pity that the chosen road was in such shocking condition — really little more than a cart track. She endured the jolting patiently, her mind many miles away in distant Yorkshire.

Presently the young man got down to open a gate, carefully securing his horses to the gatepost. It was with a sense of complete disbelief that she saw him turn back to the carriage and produce an ugly looking pistol, and heard him say, in tones that might have belonged to quite a different man, "Get down, the pair of you."

Before she had fully understood the change in the situation, Elsie broke into affronted expostulation. "This is no time for foolish jokes, Daniel. I'm downright ashamed of you. And before the mistress, too."

"No joke, my girl. Get down, before I lose my patience," he riposted grimly with a menacing jerk of the pistol, and as she still stared in disbelief he added with brutal candour, "And don't play the innocent. You know well enough what I'm after. Who told me all about her wealthy mistress and all the pretty gewgaws that she owned?"

Such a wave of shame and misery engulfed poor Elsie then that she climbed out of the carriage quite mechanically, even turning, of long habit, to help Mrs. Longden negotiate the awkwardly high step, and then stood seemingly paralysed. It was only when Pelly, having seized and examined her mistress's purse exclaimed disgustedly, "A paltry thirty guineas! Not worth the delay," and then turned on Mrs. Longden wrenching the locket from her throat that Elsie came suddenly and disastrously to life. Recklessly she flung herself at Pelly and snatched at the hand that held the gun. As he pulled the trigger, the bullet, going slightly wide, seared Mrs. Longden's cheek. He wrenched free of Elsie's hold, struck Mrs. Longden a powerful blow on the head with the empty gun, dropped it and turned his attention to the girl who was now clawing at him in impotent frenzy. Easy enough to master *her*. The sensible course would be to knock her on the head like the other one, but her fury of hatred aroused in him the lust that her simple affection had never stirred, and against his strength she was helpless. Kick and scratch and bite as she would, he would take her now. Powerful hands forced her to the ground and tore greedily at her clothing, her frantic struggles were smothered beneath the weight of his body and she was forced to endure the agony of his possession.

And then, lust and cruelty alike assuaged, he would not give her the swift death for which now she prayed. It pleased him to explain to the broken weeping creature that if ever her dealings with him were disclosed, she would face the hangman for her complicity. And lest that should not prove deterrent enough, he elaborated with convincing eloquence on the evils that would befall her if she tried to betray him, vowing that, wherever she hid, his vengeance would seek her out.

After which he produced a pocket comb and a mirror, set his appearance carefully to rights, untied the horses and drove off.

Chapter Thirteen

IT was the old shepherd, Jeff Braddock, who came upon the hapless victims of Pelly's assault. Jeff liked to look over the sheep each day. Though it was full summer and the grazing plentiful, his foolish charges could still contrive to get themselves into a variety of awkward fixes where his help was needed. Besides, since his wife had died last winter he had no one but his dog and the sheep to talk to, his cottage being too isolated to encourage the visits of his aged cronies. On this lovely summer evening he came slowly down the hill content that all was well with the flock and looking forward to the enjoyment of a tasty stew that he had left to simmer on the hob. Gyp, who had trotting sedately at her master's heels, suddenly uttered an enquiring yelp and turned off the track, striking up hill towards the old road that led to the long deserted iron workings.

The old man smiled and turned obediently in her wake. Maybe some child had strayed away from home and was lost on the hillside, for now that he was nearer he fancied he could hear a faint wailing such as a terrified child might make. With a heart that was tender to all small defenceless creatures, he hastened his steps.

The scene which met his eyes was truly shocking. One woman lay stretched insensible in the roadway, while a second was scurrying like some demented creature between the body and the roadside ditch, where she scooped up water in her hands and carried it to sprinkle on the unconscious woman's face, and all the time keeping up the eerie keening noise that he had heard from a distance.

"Now what's going on here, Missus?" drawled Jeff, in his soft countryman's voice. "Been a haccident, 'as there?"

The poor soul must have been proper startled he thought compassionately, for at the sound of his voice she uttered a dreadful shriek and made as though to run off.

"Nay, now, nay my maid," said the old man gently. "Don't 'ee run away. Old Jeff Braddock never 'urt nobody in all 'is days. Tell me what's amiss and I'll 'elp 'ee if I can. 'As the lady fainted like?"

Some note of human warmth in the kind old voice penetrated the swirling mist of horror in which poor Elsie was drifting. To his deep embarrassment she came to him in a swift little rush and fell at his feet, clasping her arms about his knees and pressing her face against his stained old moleskins while she choked out hoarsely, "Help me with her. Help my mistress. She's still alive, for her heart is beating, but I cannot bring her to her senses."

"There now, my maid," said the old man, patting the dishevelled drooping head with a gnarled but gentle hand. "Don't 'ee take on so. Just 'ee let I go, and us'll see what best to do for the poor lady. Maybe 'tis the heat of the sun has struck her down."

But when he came closer and saw the dreadful wound that disfigured the still face, he recoiled in deep dismay. Such injuries were beyond his simple skill. The bullet had struck Mrs. Longden on the jaw and ploughed an ugly powder-stained furrow across cheek and temple. But far worse than this was the head wound which must, thought old Jeff, have broken the skull. He dare not touch the deep spreading contusion, still slowly oozing blood which matted and stained the pretty hair.

"I'd best go for help, my lassie," he told the girl who gazed at him with that dumb imploring stare. She'd been in trouble too, poor lass, her mouth all cut and swollen, her arms and throat blue with bruises and her dress torn and stained. But when he suggested going for help, she began to scream and carry on like someone crazed. So far as he could make out from her distraught pleading it would be the death of her if anyone found out what had happened. He hesitated. The one on the ground was like to die any way, whatever he did. Best save the one he *could* help, and let the other poor thing take her chance. He rubbed his chin reflectively. It was half a mile to his cottage, and he had neither cart nor pony. It would have to be a carrying job. He hoped the crazy wench was strong enough to help, for he'd never manage it alone.

In the end they managed it between them, though the old man was pretty done up by the time that they had lifted Mrs. Longden on to a hurdle taken from the sheep pen and carried her by the rough track to his cottage. Elsie, now that there was something positive to be done, seemed to be imbued with new strength, and her manner, which had so alarmed him, was much calmer. He brought her fresh water from the spring and set a kettle to boil. There was only the one bed, so the injured woman was laid on that and Elsie cut away the blood matted hair and cleansed the deep wound while the old man hunted out a flannel bedgown that had belonged to his wife, and then suggested to the girl that she, too, might like to change her torn dress for one of Martha's prints.

Now that she had done all that could be done for her mistress, Elsie was fast yielding to overwhelming exhaustion. Dumbly she did as the old man suggested, even managing at his insistence to swallow a few spoonfuls of the stew, and stretched herself on the rough pallet that he had contrived for her beside her mistress.

Contrary to his expectations Mrs. Longden did not succumb to her injuries though it was three days before she showed any sign of returning consciousness. Elsie had tended her devotedly so far as the simple resources of the cottage permitted, finding some measure of healing for herself in unremitting care of her mistress. The old man watched over them both supplying their needs, asking no questions as to how they had come to be in so shocking a state and waiting patiently for the time when the girl would confide in him. That day came when she finally realised that though Mrs. Longden's physical condition was slowly improving, her mental state was not. She accepted Elsie's ministrations without comment and never enquired how it had come about that she was lying sick in the shepherd's cottage. When the girl discovered that her mistress did not recognise her an remembered nothing of her previous life, not even her own name, it had seemed to Elsie to be Fate's final blow. The old man had come in from the hill to find her weeping bitterly, and at last she had told him a little of their story, though she was still too terrified of Pelly's vengeance to give him her full confidence. The old shepherd, his simplicity as great as the girl's own, was brought to agree that her best hope of safety lay in remaining hidden.

So matters rested for several weeks until both mistress and maid were largely recovered from their physical ordeal. Mrs. Longden spoke little, spending long hours gazing blankly into the distance until Elsie felt she could endure the silence no longer. She began to wonder what was to become of the pair of them if her mistress never *did* recover the use of her faculties, linked with the realisation that it would be much easier to remain hidden if she did *not*. Close on the heels of this thought came awareness that they had been all this time a burden on the good old man who had sheltered them — had even given up his own bed for the comfort of the sick woman.

She spoke to him of these matters that night when Mrs. Longden was asleep. He hushed her smilingly when she tried to thank him. He had given much thought to their problem, he said. Though he would be loth to part with them they should not make their home with him, for he was old and could not expect to live much longer, and then what would become of them, for his master would surely want the cottage for the next shepherd. Had Elsie no family of her own to whom she could turn? She was young and strong and able for work, so she would not be a burden. He did not stress the fact that by refusing to disclose the identity of her employer or to restore her to her family, she had herself taken on a heavy burden of responsibility.

So it had come about that the two women had journeyed to York. Jeff had lent them the money to pay for seats on the stage coach, trusting to Elsie to repay him when she could. Her widowed sister had been told just sufficient of their story to frighten her into a promise of silence. There they had lived secluded. Elsie had found work as a seamstress, and she and her sister between them had cared tenderly for the afflicted woman. She had seemed content, in her placid way. But of late, said Elsie, there had been a change. She was restless, talked more, asked more questions, which they found difficult to answer. And now, tonight, she had remembered her husband's name.

This was the tale that Elsie had outlined, confessing her culpability with deep penitence and keeping back only the final bitter experience that she herself had endured at Pelly's hands. Mrs. Gordon had been grave but kind, saying that nothing could be decided until the story had been told to Mr. Longden, and saying that the girl should now go home, on the promise that she would come betimes to Coney Street next day lest her absence should distress her mistress. Then Faith had run across the room and put her arms about her. "Poor Elsie!" she had said gently. "I don't wonder you were afraid. It was dreadful for you. And you have done your best to look after Mama." And at that Elsie had broken down and wept helplessly, until at last Mrs. Gordon had sent her home in the carriage with Nurse MacNab to care for her.

*

On Clemency now devolved the task of conveying the news to her father. After the first sharp exclamation of scarce-believing joy, he heard her out in silence. But despite her careful description of her mother's injuries and parlous mental state the glow of happiness on the blind face did not fade.

Indeed when she came to the end of the story with its heartening note of hope in her mother's reference to himself by name, he could endure to sit still no longer, and sprang to his feet to pace eagerly up and down the room, avoiding familiar obstacles with practised ease.

"We must bring her home at once," he exclaimed. "I am convinced that in time she will recover completely, just as I have known all this while that she was still alive. And since it seems to have been the meeting with friends of her own standing, in a familiar setting, that has brought about this startling improvement, may it not be that the return to her own home will complete the cure?"

He fell silent again, and when next he spoke he seemed to have forgotten his daughter's presence, for he spoke softly, as though communing with himself. "And if it does not, then still I shall have my darling to worship and to cherish, and perhaps, if fate prove kind, I may win again the love she once bestowed." And his face lit to such joyous anticipation that Clemency's eyes filled with tears and she stole softly from the room with a sense that she was intruding on something too sacred for even her loving gaze to look upon, and went off to the kitchen to find Prudence and Betsy and to tell them the wonderful news. And in a secret corner of her heart she wondered if some day she might come to love and be loved as her father loved her mother.

She was not half done answering their flood of eager questions when she heard him calling her name, and then he arrived in the kitchen himself, all wild impatience to set out at once on the journey to York. "Did young Giles bring you over?" he demanded eagerly. "Ask him to procure me a chaise, and to be sure to pick four good strengthy beasts. Desire Betsy — ah! You are here Betsy. Is it not splendid news? Will you pack my night bag? It has but just struck four. I can be in York before midnight if we put ourselves about."

It called for considerable eloquence to persuade him that it would be wiser to defer his journey until the next day; that he could scarcely travel alone so far from home, but that either Piers or Giles would gladly bear him company; and finally that it would be foolish to hire a turnout that was sure to be inferior when all the resources of the Manor stables were at his disposal.

To most of this he eventually submitted, since it would help to speed the meeting with his wife, but it took Betsy's sourly sensible comment, that a midnight arrival was just the thing to startle a delicate lady into a serious set-back, to make him abandon the idea of setting out at once, and reluctantly consent to an early morning start.

Within the hour his daughters were heartily wishing that he had been allowed to have his way. They had become so accustomed to his gentle acceptance of *their* plans, that to find him taking command of his household with the full force of masculine vigour, issuing strings of orders with a crisp intonation that brooked no argument, was quite a stunning shock. They were kept in a breathless bustle until Lady Eleanor, prompted by the sympathetic Giles, arrived in the carriage and insisted on bearing them all off with her to dinner.

Since she had brought with her two sturdy wenches who had been straitly enjoined to scrub and polish every corner of Mrs. Longden's apartments until they were fit to receive her again, her husband allowed himself to be persuaded and his exhausted family sank back thankfully into the comfortable carriage while their father lingered for a last word with a very weary and distinctly crusty Betsy, reiterating the list of favourite dishes that must be prepared against his wife's return, and the names of several delicacies, unobtainable locally, that must be listed for purchase in York. Betsy listened and assented with laudable patience, having already received the same instructions twice, and, as she grumbled to Elspeth when the door had finally close behind him, "As though I did not know as well as the next one just how the mistress likes things done! But there — it is good to see him so happy."

Elspeth's industry and quiet ways had won favour with Betsy. She even allowed that with careful teaching and supervision — her own, of course — the lass might some day make a cook. Now, settling her aching limbs in the old rocker before the kitchen fire, she actually permitted her to brew a posset, the while she held forth on the enticing prospect of promotion to kitchen maid, if Lady Eleanor could be persuaded to release her to Mrs. Longden's service when Ash Croft was restored to its former dignity and comfort. And Elspeth, who felt that an inside knowledge of the most stirring and romantic event that had occurred in the village during her short lifetime was in itself sufficient reward for her humble services, listened and stirred and wondered if Will was enjoying the meat pasty that she had saved from her own dinner to give to him. Not that he went hungry, he had told her, during that stolen interview behind the poultry house. His new masters fed him well enough. But she didn't like the sound of the job. Why must he lie hid, if they were honest horse dealers? More likely horse thieves, and Will one that was all too easy led astray.

It was fortunate that dinner with Lady Eleanor was not a formal occasion, since Mr. Longden was for ever breaking across each promising conversational topic to ask his girls to remind him of some additional luxury that must be obtained to ensure their mother's comfort. There was an animated discussion with Lady Eleanor firmly insisting that it was quite absurd to be buying lengths of linen and silk and velvet. Mrs. Longden would very much prefer to make her own choice. He explained that Clemency had given away a great many of his wife's clothes, saying that they were old fashioned and Mama would need new ones.

"Yes. And so she will," agreed Lady Eleanor briskly. "But not tomorrow. We females like to take time over the choosing of our gowns. They are not bought at random you must understand, but are planned to sort well with our bonnets and cloaks, or, in the case of an evening gown, to set off our jewels."

Mr. Longden clapped a hand to his head. "Jewels!" he exclaimed in sharp dismay. "I had clean forgot! I was to have seen Gregson — the fellow from Rundell and Bridge — this evening, and in all the excitement it went quite out of my head. Dear me! How extremely remiss. Especially as the poor man has had that wearisome journey for nothing. How would it be if we carried him to York with us Piers? It would save him a fully day's travelling, for he could take the London Mail from there. That would make some small amends. But he must be at Ash Croft betimes, for I will not stay for him!"

Piers offered to have a message of explanation and apology carried to the jeweller, and the company were able to address themselves to the excellent dinner to which they had been so unceremoniously bidden. Mr. Longden emerging from one of his fits of abstraction to request his hostess to compliment her cook on the fricassee of game.

"It is one of my favourite dishes," he explained, innocently unaware that the remark had reduced his two younger daughters to suppressed giggles, while the third, with heightened colour and a brilliant sparkle in her eye, devoted herself to a helping of roast duck with pensive dignity. Lady Eleanor, aware of some undercurrent, looked slightly puzzled, but was too well bred to enquire into what was clearly a private joke, and returned her attention to Mr. Longden, pleasing him very much by telling him how grateful she was to Clemency for helping her these past weeks, and paying a graceful tribute to the girl by commending her capabilities in just such moderate and sensible terms as carried far more conviction than fulsome praise.

Mr. Longden beamed delightedly and said what a comfort the child would be to her Mama, and Clemency felt herself to be quite the horridest creature in all Nature because she could not welcome the prospect with wholehearted delight. Piers, setting down her subdued mien to embarrassment at the public praise, turned the subject by saying that he hoped she would still be able to spare a little time to help him with his letters, declaring that although his hand was now practically as good as new, he had discovered the luxury of having the tedious task performed for him, and would not lightly forego it.

The party broke up early, since the travellers meant to be up at crack of dawn, and Lady Eleanor said that Faith too, should go early to bed. Nor were her sisters reluctant to retire after their exhausting day, though one of them lay long awake, wondering how it was that a world in which all one's long cherished hopes seemed about to come true at last should seem so utterly devoid of zest and enchantment.

Chapter Fourteen

"THERE'S something wrong with the whole set-up," complained Pelly sourly. "There was no word of this last night, or my pretty Peg would have told me of it."

"Well 'er telling *me* come about quite natural like," placated Harry. "I woke up uncommon dry — must have been the pigs' fry we 'ad for supper — so I went down to the tap room for a sup of ale to wet me gullet. And Peg just 'appens to say as 'ow the bloke 'ad loped off an hour gone. But all's bowman," he added hurriedly, seeing the lowering scowl on Pelly's face, "'cos it was this 'ere Ash Croft place that 'e was going to."

Pelly grunted but his brow cleared slightly. "Maybe they're just playing it clever," he brooded, and fell silent.

Harry knew better than to interrupt this reverie with any ideas of his own about Gregson's unexpected move. He did not see how the fellow could have got wind of their plans. They had kept well out of his ken during his stay at the inn, though this precaution had not been necessary, the poor gentleman having gone immediately to his bedchamber and remained there, suffering, said Peg, from some kind of sickness brought on by the swaying of the coach. Harry had set eyes on him only once, and a puny undersized little fellow he was. *He* would present no problem in a hold up. A good hearty sneeze would just about blow him away, and one could no more imagine him carrying a pistol or a knife than one could picture him, Harry, figged out in silk stockings and satin breeches at a Court ball.

The amiable grin with which he welcomed this exotic flight of fancy was wiped clean away by Pelly's brusque, "And what cause have you to grin, gapeseed? Seems to me there's little cause for grinning in the prospect of losing a fortune."

Harry mumbled something apologetic as how he'd only been thinking that there Mr. Gregson wouldn't show to much advantage if it came to fisticuffs.

"It's not like to do so unless we can guess what he plans to do next," said Pelly. "If he's not coming back here, where does he plan to board the London Mail? For we must nobble him before then. It takes four at least to

94

stop the Mail, and likely lads at that" — with a disparaging glance at Harry.

Further discussion revealed the depressing fact that there were no less than three different points at which the intending traveller might choose to board the coach, and it was clearly impossible for two men and a 'half wit' as Pelly described Will Overing, to cover all of them.

"There's only the one thing to be done," decided Pelly at last. "The one road that he's bound to use is the lane that runs easterly from Ash Croft to the turnpike."

"The one that passes that stud farm? The Manor 'ouse?" asked Harry helpfully.

Pelly nodded impatiently. "Yes. Though we take him before he gets that far. About half a mile from Ash Croft the lane goes up a steepish hill with a sharp bend at the top, and there's a spinney on the left where we can lie close till he comes. If my memory serves me, we can cover the gates of Ash Croft from the hill top and make sure of our man. This is one time when we don't want to be stopping any chance-come chaise.

"We'll maybe have a long wait," said Harry dubiously.

"So I suppose we should sit here by the parlour fire and send a message to Mr. Gregson to kindly let us know when he's ready to leave," snapped Pelly. "If we've to keep watch all day *and* all night, I'm having those sparklers." And then, in rare condescension, "Don't you see, Harry, they're just the right stamp for men of our calling? Good class stuff, but commonplace. What's the good of taking the Norton diamonds or the Eversley black pearls — even if so be as you could come nigh either? You can't sell them. They've to go to a fence and be broken up — and away goes the profit. Now this little lot — why, Barney'll place every piece with some of these new-come-up mushrooms that made a fortune in the war. No questions asked and everybody happy. That's the way to make easy money, Harry boy."

Harry regarded him with admiration, and then, encouraged by his unusual affability, ventured a question. "You seem uncommon well acquainted with these 'ere sparklers, Dan'l?"

Pelly grinned. "So I am, Harry, so I am. I near as nothing had a touch at them once before, but it came to naught through one of those mischances that happen to the best of us." For a moment his mind went back to that Surrey hillside where he had slain the mistress and despoiled the maid. The grin widened over that last memory. He wondered where the wench was now, and whether she still went in fear of his vengeance. A pity he had never come up with her again. She had been his first virgin. It might have been amusing to make her dance to his piping. Then he dismissed the thought as idle folly when there was business to be done.

"I'll settle our reckoning, Harry. Do you get out to the Wyke barn and bring Overing and Lucifer to the spinney. Best let the lad ride the stallion — he'll go quietly for him. I'll join you as soon as I've set all straight here."

At much the same time that this conference was taking place, the Longden twins were also discussing their plans for the immediate future, with Clemency curled up on the end of Pru's bed while her sister folded and put away her clean linen. Pru had a good deal to tell, for though Giles had not yet spoken to her father and their affairs must now wait upon his return, they had agreed matters to their own entire satisfaction and neither of them really doubted that parental approval would be forthcoming. Clemency wished her sister happy and tried to take what comfort she could from the thought that at least Pru would be living no further away than the Manor. This put her in mind of the fact that Giles was only his cousin's steward, and she enquired with sisterly candour whether he was in a position to support a wife.

Thereupon Pru poured out the whole tale of Captain Kennedy's generosity, and how Giles was to step into his cousin's shoes. For her own part she could not understand a man choosing to resign such a comfortable heritage as the Manor in favour of adventuring in strange and distant lands, which must, by all accounts, be very dangerous, as well as horridly uncomfortable. But it seemed that Captain Kennedy *was* so constituted, and — she blushed — had heartily approved his cousin's decision to marry, and even his choice of bride. Matters were already in train for the transfer of the estate to its new owner. Perhaps — shyly — they might be married in the spring, if Mama was well enough for all the excitement of a wedding.

Clemency listened and exclaimed and sympathised, saying all that was proper, with a lonely little ache in her heart as of a child shut out from a party yet compelled to watch the glowing happiness within. Presently, when Pru had come to an end of her plans, she said casually, "Will Captain Kennedy not return to England, then? Does he intend to reside wholly in Australia?"

Pru explained the arrangement about the Dower House but said that certainly he seemed to regard Australia as his home. Then, sensitive as always to her twin's mood, said thoughtfully, "It is a pity that you should have taken him in such dislike at your first meeting. I would have thought the pair of you well suited, for you have always yearned for travel and adventure. Strange how our looks belie us." She studied their two reflections in the mirror. "You, so dainty and feminine, as though you should sit for ever on a cushion and sew a fine seam, with courtiers attending your every whim, while I look the complete Amazon, and all I want is Giles and" — her voice dropped to a shy tenderness — "his children."

Clemency didn't answer. She was envisaging a busy and useful future as a comfort to Mama and spinster aunt to those same children, and finding the prospect little to her taste. Children had not come much in her way until the advent of the Gordons, but of late she, too, had sometimes dreamed of a child, a dark haired lad with laughing blue eyes, an upstanding scamp, mischievous perhaps, but gallant and gay and loving.

Pru cut sharply across the little silence. "What *did* go wrong? That day you went to ask Piers to help us? You never told me the whole story. Was he unkind to you? Too high and mighty?"

"No, indeed," said Clemency promptly, for fair was fair and he had been neither. Too attentive would be nearer the mark, but that was a secret she would keep to herself. "He behaved as if I were too young and silly to be out without my nurse," she said at last.

Pru looked puzzled. "I suppose you would dislike being condescended to," she said doubtfully. "But surely you do not still hold it against him?"

Clemency tilted her chin. "I cannot see why you are refining so much on such a trivial matter. Captain Kennedy and I are perfectly good friends. Must you try your hand at match making, just because you are happily in love? I think I am not yet at my last prayers, and may yet hope to find a partner to my liking." And then, swiftly penitent, "I'm sorry, Pru, love. Set my ill humour down to too much excitement yesterday — for indeed I feel horridly flat and dull today. And though I am truly happy for you and Giles you cannot expect me to give you up to him without a little selfish moan. I'll smile and dance at your wedding, I promise!" And a quick loving hug dispelled any soreness that the snub might have left behind.

By tacit consent the subject of Piers Kennedy was dropped and the sisters spent the rest of the day in looking over Mrs. Longden's furs and hanging them in the fresh air to sweeten, and then in pressing out and furbishing up their own gowns, so that Mama should not find her daughters too dreadfully shabby.

"You will not mind being left alone tonight?" asked Clemency, as Betsy came in to draw the curtains and shut out the fading daylight. "Giles was to collect the letters from the receiving office on his way home, and I promised Captain Kennedy that I would deal with any that required an answer. But I can come back after I have finished the letters if you will be nervous on your own."

"Goose!" smiled Pru. "What should I be afraid of? With Betsy and Elspeth and Lady Eleanor's two girls, it seems to me I have guardian angels a-plenty! There's Giles now." She got up to bring Clemency's cloak, fastening the strings at the throat and settling the hood snugly with gentle fingers that expressed her deep affection better than any words, and even stooped to brush a light kiss on her sister's cheek, a rare caress in an undemonstrative family. She watched the gig out of sight, shivered in the raw November air, and turned back to the comfort of the hearth.

In the spinney at the top of the hill, Harry pulled his coat collar higher and stamped his feet in an effort to bring some warmth to those frozen members.

"Quiet, man!" hissed Pelly. "Listen!"

Carried on the frosty air came clear enough the sound of hoofs and wheels. Straining his eyes through the gathering dusk he could just make out the shape of a vehicle drawing out of the gates of Ash Croft. And yes! there were two occupants, a big husky looking fellow driving, and a smaller one beside him.

"At last!" he breathed exultantly. "That'll be them. And about time, too. The little'un'll be Gregson. Do you tend to him, Harry, while I take the driver, and you, lad," to the pallid faced Will, "go to the horse's head as soon as I've stopped 'em."

Harry was across the lane in a swift silent dash that contrasted sharply with his earlier noisy demonstration, crouching in the frozen ditch and melting out of sight among a clump of low growing bushes. Pelly swung into the saddle and held his pistol ready, hoping for once that he would not need to fire, since the sound, so close to human habitation, might summon help to his victims.

The gig came on at a gentle pace. The rise was steep and Giles was ever careful of his horses. Fully engaged in watching for hazards in the ill-surfaced lane and never dreaming of danger so close to home, the surprise when it came was complete. At one moment the hill was bare and peaceful, at the next a great black stallion leapt out of the hedge as though it must crash into the gig, to be pulled up, rearing up above his head while a loud voice yelled at him to stop and a pistol was levelled at his head. As, instinctively, he swerved to his left, another figure leapt up from the nearside ditch and sprang catlike towards Clemency, while yet a third appeared to catch at Chevalier's head. Outmanoeuvred and outnumbered, Giles cut furiously at the mounted man with his whip. The fellow evaded the onslaught, wrenched the black aside, and rose in his stirrups, reversing the gun to bring it down in a heavy blow aimed at Giles's head. It was fortunate for Giles that in the instant of its descent Clemency pulled him back with all her strength, so that the weapon struck him only a glancing blow on the side of his head and expended its full force on his shoulder. Clemency saw him sway and topple awkwardly from his seat almost beneath the hoofs of the frantic stallion, but at that moment Harry succeeded in getting a foothold on the hub of the wheel and dragged her roughly to the ground.

It was Harry's sharp exclamation of disbelieving fury that drew Pelly's attention from Giles and brought him round to Harry's side of the vehicle before the stallion could vent its fury on the limp body so perilously close.

Harry was shaking the helpless girl like a rag doll, pouring out the while a stream of blasphemous vituperation that his captive was not the little jeweller but a useless wench. Pelly stared — for a moment unable to believe that his plan had so miscarried; that the elaborate trap had caught only a pair of silly country lovers, for so he deemed them. Then his attention was caught by something familiar about the frightened white face framed in the loose goldbrown hair, for the hood had fallen back in Harry's rough handling. Perhaps — the idea came to him — it was just possible that all was not yet lost. "Let her be, Harry," he said, quietly enough, though his fingers bit into Harry's shoulder with bruising force. The girl reeled away, sick and dizzy, to clutch at the side of the gig for support. Pelly studied her curiously. Yes — despite shabby cloak and simple gown, there was definitely an air of quality.

"Who is she?" he snapped. "Either of you know her?"

It was Will Overing who answered. Will had played his part as bidden. He had seen the blow that had struck down Master Giles — as decent a chap as ever stepped, allowing for him being one of the swells — and his heart had turned to water within him. He longed only to be free of his new associates. But he dare not go against them.

"'Tis Miss Longden," he muttered sullenly, "Miss Clemency," and turned his face away from her, though she had not so much as glanced his way.

Pelly nodded. So his half guess at the girl's identity had been right. "Then maybe we're not done for yet," he said thoughtfully. "Search that fellow I laid out, Harry, and make sure there's naught hid in the gig."

It did not take Harry long to report that there was nothing of value save a few coins in the young fellow's pocket and a gold watch, which trophies he handed over with a deeply disgruntled mien. He then asked if he should search the wench, who had managed to stumble to Giles's side and was feeling for a pulse beat with shaking fingers. Pelly shook his head. "No need," he said. "We'll take her along with us. The old man can have her back when he hands over the jewels — or the money if he's already sold 'em. I reckon they were worth a cool ten thousand. That shall be the lady's price — and I'll warrant he'll pay up willingly enough to have his dainty ewe lamb restored to him unharmed."

Harry heartily approved. Never at a loss, wasn't Dan. Trust him to snatch victory out of defeat. But he was anxious about their exposed position on the open hillside. Could they not withdraw to some more sheltered spot to settle the final details?

Pelly swung down from his horse. "Here, lad," he called sharply to the miserable Will. "The bay'll stand quiet enough now. Take this brute. And look smart about it," he added, glancing keenly at the scared face and reluctant approach.

Will did as he was told, wishing that he had the courage to make a break for it, and knowing that to do so would be to invite a bullet in the back.

Pelly stooped over the prostrate Giles. Clemency had loosened his neckcloth and was staunching the blood that trickled down his face with an inadequate handkerchief.

"Just let him be, Mistress Longden," advised a suave voice over her shoulder. "He's taken little harm and is coming round already, and since I happen to want him alive he'll continue to do well enough, for just so long as *you* do exactly as you're told."

Clemency looked up fearfully. "What do you w-want?" she faltered. "I have no money, no, nor jewels either."

"As if your pretty self isn't worth more than a bagful of golden guineas," said Pelly smoothly, and smiled to see terror flicker in the brown eyes. "I'm sure your Papa will think so, and will gladly reward me for bringing you safe home. So it's into the gig with you, my dear, and not a squeak out of those pretty lips, mind, whoever we chance to meet, or I fear things will go ill with your poor young friend here. Now where's that stupid oaf got to? Go fetch him, Harry boy, and the two of you get our young gentleman out of sight. Tie him up and stop his mouth. I'll take the lad with me, or like as not he'll lope off. If I'm not back within two hours —" he tossed over Giles's watch — "cut the fellow's throat and roll him into the ditch." His eyes flickered sideways at Clemency to make sure that this threat had gone home. She looked like a creature turned to stone, realising to the full Giles's deadly danger and her own helplessness. If she did not submit — if any accident should delay them — then Giles would die. Somehow she forced her shaking limbs to obey her will and climbed into the gig, waiting numbly for her captor to join her.

But it was the lad who clambered into the driving seat and took the reins, urging the placid bay to a steady trot, while the highwayman ranged alongside after a moment or two in the fashion of an attentive escort. By the time they emerged from the lane on to the turnpike it was full dark. They had met no one. Even had they done so, Clemency would not have dared cry out for help.

There was a snapped order, and the pace picked up sharply on the better road. She could only be grateful. There was no time, as yet, to dwell on her own desperate situation. All her mind was set on preserving Giles's life. It was a humble terrified girl who did all she was bid with pathetic alacrity, climbing the steep ladder to the stable loft that was to be her prison, even holding out her hands for the bonds for which Pelly apologised with oily gallantry. It would not be for long, he assured her, tightening the leather straps about her wrists beyond all possibility of escape and then passing a broader strap about her waist which he secured to a wall staple with a padlock; just until he had arranged that her unfortunate beau should carry the news of her capture and the demand for ransom to the proper quarters. Then he would return and she could be more comfortably established. Meanwhile he need not subject her to the discomfort of a gag, since there was no one to hear however loud she shouted. With that he left her, and within minutes she heard the gig drive off. She could only pray that he might come safely to his rendezvous.

Chapter Fifteen

"IT was the most touching thing I think I ever saw," said Piers quietly.

"She knew him at once?" marvelled Lady Eleanor.

"Just raised her head from her embroidery, and warned him, as she might have done in her own drawing-room, 'Take care, love, there is a work table between you and the hearth. I will show you,' and went to take his hand and lead him to the couch as though they had never been parted."

"And he?"

"Is a brave man, and a wise one. He made no great outcry, just took her in his arms and kissed her gently, a devoted husband newly come to join his wife on a visit to friends, and talked to her of small domestic matters, of the girls and Betsy and the commodities that Betsy had commissioned him to obtain while he was in York. She laughed at that, and said they would go shopping as soon as he was rested from the tiresome journey."

"It would seem that she is perfectly recovered."

Piers shook his head. "No; for she asks no questions but simply accepts everything as it comes, and when she is surprised or puzzled she just smiles and says she must have forgotten. But I would hope that her complete recovery is only a matter of time, and perhaps of familiar surroundings."

"How did Faith take it all?"

Piers smiled. "A little distressed, I fear, for it was pretty evident that her Mama did not recognise *her*, though it was passed off as being due to the change in her appearance from schoolgirl to young lady. But they are off to London tomorrow and Aunt Chloe set her to packing which helped to raise her spirits."

"And when may we expect the Longdens home? The girls and Betsy will be anxious to know."

"Not for some days I understand. Mr. Longden was all for removing to the Swan, not wishing to be a charge on his friends, but Aunt Chloe and Cousin Marjorie between them persuaded him that it would be better for his wife if they remained quietly in Coney Street, since she had so readily accepted the notion that they were visiting friends. I thought I would drive over to Ash Croft after dinner and give them the news."

He had not stopped to change his riding-dress before seeking out his aunt, and now straightened his long length with the air of a man pleasantly tired after a day of strenuous open air activity. "I left the chaise at the disposal of the Longdens," he explained, "and rode back, as I knew you would all be eager to hear the outcome. Has Miss Longden been in today?"

Lady Eleanor said she had not. "Giles spoke of bringing her back with him but he is not yet returned. Doubtless he is still lingering at Ash Croft, and time is forgotten."

There was a sympathetic twinkle in her eyes and Piers smiled back at her. "*That* affair is happily settled, I take it?" he asked.

"Well Giles did not quite like to approach Mr. Longden just at this juncture, but yes, certainly it is as good as settled. They hope to be married in the spring. Giles means to ask you if you cannot delay your departure so that you can be his groomsman."

Piers thought it unlikely that he would still be in Yorkshire for the happy occasion, but admitted that so far he had not been able to arrange a passage. They were deep in friendly argument over the conflicting claims of business interests and family loyalty when Mattie tapped at the door and informed her mistress that a message had just been brought up from the stables asking if Captain Kennedy would go across there as soon as possible.

"Who wants me?" asked Piers in surprise, for the stables were more properly his cousin's province. At the same moment Lady Eleanor said, "Something amiss with one of the horses, I suppose. Is Master Giles there, Mattie?"

"Yes, ma'am," said Mattie stolidly, but volunteered no further information.

"Then I'll go now," said Piers, "before I put off those exceedingly dirty leathers. You spoil us, Aunt Nell. Most ladies would object to my very odorous presence. I will remove myself at once," and he sauntered out of the room with an affectionate grin at her laughing disclaimer.

He found Mattie waiting for him as he closed the drawing-room door. "I didn't want to say anything as 'ud upset her ladyship," she said low-voiced. "The truth is that Master Giles is a bit knocked up. Must have been an accident of some sort. Jerry's sent for the doctor, but young master was urgent to speak with you. Working himself into a proper stew he was, so best to hurry, Sir."

Piers needed no second telling. And the scene that met his eyes as he strode into the harness room was sufficiently startling. Seeing the young master wavering and swaying as he came in, one of the lads had rushed helpfully forward and put an arm about his waist, at the same time drawing the injured right arm over his own shoulders. This well meant effort at support had proved disastrous. Giles, still sick and giddy from the blow on his head, succumbed to the stab of agony from a broken collar bone so rudely handled, and collapsed in a sprawling heap on the floor. Piers came in to find one groom frantically splashing water in his master's face, while old Jerry was adjuring the abashed youngster to "give over mauling the poor lad, do, and be off up to the house for a sup of brandy for 'im. And make sure as you don't alarm the Missus."

Accustomed to dealing with injuries of varying degrees, a brief examination assured Piers that his cousin's were not desperate, despite the shocking appearance of greenish pallor and bruised and bloodstained face. The tale of his sudden collapse was quickly told and its cause established. He was made as comfortable as possible in a chair hastily brought from Jerry's quarters, the injured arm secured to his body to prevent further damage, and a glass of brandy thrust into his left hand, while his cousin cleansed and bound up the head wound, sternly bidding him hold his tongue the while and promising that he should tell his tale at leisure once his hurts had been looked to.

"You *must* listen, Piers," he burst out, jerking his head away from the sponge. "'Twasn't just a spill. D'you think I should care for that? I tell you it was a hold-up. From what was said later is seems they'd expected us to be carrying jewels — God knows why — in a gig — on a country lane! And when they were disappointed of the expected haul they made off with Clemency."

The steady swabbing of the sponge checked for a moment, then was methodically resumed. Giles, expecting a wrathful outburst of comment and blame, repeated impatiently, "Don't you understand? They've abducted her and are holding her to ransom. In fact" — a wry grimace twisted his pleasant features — "the sneering devil who carried her off was good enough to inform me that I owed my life to her submission and to the fact that they needed me as a messenger. Said that for his own part he wasn't so set on the Quality, but 'the pretty little lady' was counting on me to bring her off safe. Then I was bundled into my own gig like a whipped puppy and told to make haste home." He groaned, and put up his good arm to shield his face.

"Steady, lad," said Piers quietly. "Fretting and fuming'll do no good. Save your strength, for I'm going to need your help. Just let's have you a bit more presentable and then we'll take counsel with my aunt. Yes" — to Giles's surprised grunt — "she'll have to know. It can't be hid. Sit still and finish that brandy and I'll go warn her of the pickle you're in, or we shall have *her* fainting away next."

He called to Jerry to direct the physician to the house when he arrived. "Let Mr. Giles sit quietly for ten minutes or so, and then bring him up to the house yourself. He'll manage it, I think, with a shoulder to lean on."

Striding through the quiet dark, he permitted his thoughts to turn for one brief moment to Clemency, small, sweet Clemency, so proud and so plucky. Where was she now, and how would they use her, brutes so debased that they would abduct a woman — a mere child — in their greed for gold? His mouth set in a line that boded ill for any who harmed her. Yet as he had bidden Giles, so he himself must control the murderous rage that seethed within him. Cold, reasoned planning was what was needed first. Time enough, when they had brought her off safe, to give that fury free rein.

As gently as he might he broke the news of the evening's disaster to his aunt, not making light of Giles's injuries, but warning her that Giles himself would certainly do so. "For you will find," he concluded, "that he blames himself for Miss Longden's abduction, and it will break his heart if we exclude him from our rescue bid."

Lady Eleanor's lips twisted ruefully, but she knew very well that Piers had gauged his cousin's reactions to a nicety. "Very well, my dear," she submitted. "But you will have a care to him, won't you? Hampered by the injuries he received tonight, he will be very vulnerable, and he is all I have." She turned away sharply, fearful of being betrayed into tears, thankful that at that moment Giles was carefully ushered into the room by a protective Jerry and that she could make a great show of scolding the pair of them for not coming straight to her in the first case.

Giles, installed in a high backed chair that supported his injured shoulder, his colour gradually returning to normal, was now subjected to a searching interrogation with regard to all the details of the attack, and in particular the length of time that had elapsed before the leader of the gang had returned to the scene of the outrage. That was of special importance, explained Piers, because it limited the distance to which the captive could have been carried.

"Unless they simply handed her over to a waiting accomplice," suggested Lady Eleanor gloomily.

But Piers judged this to be unlikely, since it seemed that abduction had only been decided upon when the original scheme of robbery had failed.

Giles was able to be quite specific on the time factor, since Harry, carefully studying Giles's own timepiece, had announced in jocular tones that the young feller had saved his bacon by just five minutes. "Two hours you said, guv'nor, and near as nothing, two hours it is."

That was when Pelly had seen fit to inform the bound and battered Giles that he had the young lady to thank for his life. She had quite seen the force of the argument and had submitted willingly to bonds and captivity for his sake. Had she resisted — a shrug, elaborated by Harry who drew a finger across his throat in gruesome pantomime.

Piers was already bending over a tithe map which he had brought in from the estate office, his face hidden from the others as he listened to Giles filling in the details of his first bald account. They did not see his reaction to the thought of his brave child coerced into meek submission by such threats. For a moment it had seemed to him that the lines of the map were obscured and wavering before his gaze, so urgent was the thirst for vengeance that consumed him. But the voice in which he presently announced that he reckoned Chevalier could have covered from sixteen to twenty miles in the time was coolly factual; the hand that traced a wide circle on the map with the fatal spinney at its centre was perfectly steady.

Giles felt that the estimate was about right. One had to allow for the darkness, but the bay had been quite fresh and no doubt the rogues would have pressed him to the limit. They set about the disheartening task of listing all the places within a radius of twelve miles of the spinney where a prisoner might be hidden. The result was intimidating. In a district which for years had seen the growing drift of population to the towns, there was a dismayingly long list of derelict farm cottages and disused buildings which might well have been put to such a use. To search them all would be a formidable task.

"Even if we raise the alarm in the village and set every man in the place to search, it would take a week to cover all these," said Lady Eleanor despairingly. "We cannot leave that poor child to endure so long. We shall have to pay whatever ransom they demand."

"Ten thousand pounds, Mama?" enquired Giles bitterly. "We could not raise the half of such a sum. Nor could her father, I fear, in the time we are like to be allowed."

"I'm afraid it is not just a question of being able to raise the necessary sum," said Piers grimly. "If it were, we would somehow contrive between us. But in dealing with scum of this kind there can be no relying on their word. They are quite capable of collecting the ransom and still despatching their victim, lest she should recognise and denounce them on some future occasion. And unfortunately we run the same risk if we press our search too closely. I would not give much for Miss Longden's chances of survival if they imagined that we had discovered their hiding place."

Such a possibility had not occurred to his aunt. "But that means that we can do nothing at all, Piers. Surely you do not intend to sit idle while Clemency is in their hands?"

"Of course not. But we must thoroughly understand the danger that threatens before we move. And when we *do* move, we must be lightning swift."

"Very well," sighed his aunt. "What do you want us to do?"

"Giles was told we could have a week in which to raise the money, by which time they will have sent word as to how and where it is to be paid. During that week we will search the district that we have marked, but with the utmost discretion for fear of alarming our birds. There can be no question of mounting a massive search. One thing that disturbs me greatly is that there *must* be a confederate in the locality. How else could they know that Longden, despite his apparent poverty, was in possession of valuable jewellery, and that he was considering disposing of it?"

Giles passed his good hand over an aching brow. "I'm sorry to seem such a slow-top, cousin. It must be so, of course. I see it all quite plain when you explain it to me, but I confess I should never have thought of it myself. 'Twill be best if you do the thinking and planning, and I'll obey orders. What do we do first?"

At that Piers gave a genuine chuckle. "You won't like your first orders, my lad, but you've given your word. When the doctor has seen to that shoulder of yours, you're going to bed. Whether you know it or not, you've a touch of concussion from that knock on the head, which is why you're a self-confessed slow-top. A night between sheets will work wonders for you, and you'll be fit for duty tomorrow. No — don't argue — you're under orders now. Listen instead to what I want you to do tomorrow. Somewhere in this vicinity are three men and a girl who have to be fed. Take your mother with you, and visit any places where food may be bought — shops, farms, inns — though you'd better not take your mother there! Buy something — Aunt Eleanor must invent a plausible tale — and see if you can pick up any hint of strangers in the district buying supplies."

At this point Mattie came in to say that the doctor was come at last and that she had shown him up to Master Giles's room, so the conference broke up.

Piers, returning to bid his aunt good night after delivering his cousin over to the doctor's hands, found her weeping softly.

"It's that poor child," she said apologetically. "And we can do nothing."

"Recollect that she is valuable to them," said Piers with a confidence that he did not feel. "They will not harm her while there is hope of collecting the ransom."

His aunt choked on a repressed sob, but her face brightened a little. "Bless you, Piers. You always know how to comfort one. I will try to remember that. And you? You must be quite worn out. Promise me that you, too, will try to snatch some sleep."

"There is certainly nothing else that I can do before daylight," he said wearily. "It's so simple, Aunt Nell, to give good advice to others. Not quite so easy to follow it oneself." He stooped and kissed her cheek. "Pray for her," he said softly, and left the house.

Chapter Sixteen

PELLY was in no particular hurry to release his prisoner. He and Harry went in to the mouldering kitchen, leaving Will to stable the horses, with strict orders not to approach the girl or answer her if she called out to him. They then indulged in a brisk quarrel over Dan's refusal to permit Harry to kindle a fire. A candle they *must* have, but there was to be no fire to betray them by its smoke or its lingering traces. Harry cursed vigorously, stamped his feet and swung his arms and vowed they were more like to be betrayed by three hard frozen corpses, but Dan would not be moved. Will came in, blowing on numbed fingers, and began to bring food out of an old meal chest, left behind by the original owners as being too heavy to be removed.

As Will had told his cousin Elspeth, his new employers fed him well. Tonight, for some reason, and despite his long fast, the food did not tempt him. He watched the other two dispose of a giblet pie, and when Harry began to carve a knuckle of ham, Will took a piece of bread and ate a few mouthfuls of bread and ham, but with so little appetite that Pelly scowled across at him and said, in the contemptuous drawl that he reserved for Will, "Squeamish, Booberkin? You've seen naught yet. Wait till you see how we treat those that think to play us false. Such a one would be thankful for swift death before we'd done with him. Aye, and beg for it, if so be as he had a tongue left to beg with." But since Will only looked sullenly down at his boots and went on stolidly munching bread and ham, he abandoned the attempt to get a rise out of the boy and applied himself instead to the gin bottle which Harry had just brought out.

Much strengthened by this revivifying cordial, he rubbed the grease from his mouth with the back of his hand, lit a stump of candle in an old stable lantern, and announced his intention of loosing the prisoner's bonds. "And you'd best bring her some of that bread and ham," he said to Harry in an afterthought. "Don't want her dying on our hands, do we, the pretty dear. Worth nothing to us dead, and she's just the miserable poor spirited sort of creature that 'ud up and die on us just for spite."

There was no harm in letting the wench sweat a bit over her lover's fate, he thought, climbing the ladder in leisurely fashion. "Twould but make her the more biddable. He hung the lantern on a hook and freed the girl's hands before he answered the agonised question in the dark eyes.

"Yes, my dear. All went smooth as cream. Your young man went off to collect your price, just as meek and good as *you* was. You've naught to worry your pretty head about."

Since she could not imagine how he could profit by lying to her, she accepted the statement about Giles as basically true, and ignored the insolent familiarity of the man's attitude, merely turning aside her head in disgust when he put his arms about her to come at the padlock which secured her to the wall. He need not have subjected her to this particular indignity — he could have reached the padlock much more handily from the side — but it amused him to see her shrinking revulsion from the enforced contact with his body, and being now full-fed and with time on his hands, he was in the mood for entertainment. So as the hasp opened and he released the strap he kept one arm about her waist, pushed up her chin roughly with the other, and said brazenly, "And how about a kiss for the bringer of such good tidings?" and fastened his greedy mouth over hers.

Never was a man so surprised. Relieved of the paralysing fear for Giles, Clemency was herself again, no longer prepared to submit meekly to insult and mishandling. Up came one hand to deliver a resounding slap across the grinning face, and as he involuntarily jerked his head away, small white teeth drew blood from the marauding hand that had begun to fondle her throat.

He drew back for a moment and gaped in amazement at the young termagant who had so suddenly taken the place of his docile captive. Then a wide amused grin curled the red mouth. "You young vixen!" he said, half admiringly. "And me to think there was no spirit in you! Well now, if that's to be the way of it, come on my lass, and we'll see who wins. Come to think of it, I've never sampled a quality maid. 'Twill be a new experience," and with a swift pounce caught her in his arms again.

She fought him desperately, with all her small strength, kicking at his legs and pounding at his chest and head with puny fists, to his huge delight. He had twisted one hand in her hair, holding her easily at arms' length, and now as he forced her back against the wall his free hand wrenched away her cloak and tugged impatiently at the neck of her gown with intent to rip it from her shoulders. She was almost done, her breath coming in moaning gasps, the flailing hands dropping weakly to her sides, though still she struggled to twist away from him. And then, in the very moment of defeat, her fingers touched cold iron and clasped themselves about the padlock. In his careless contempt, Pelly had not bothered to close the hasp. It slid sweetly into her hand, reviving her spirit and strength. With a flash of desperate feminine cunning she closed her eyes and swayed towards him. Assured of victory he released his grip on her hair and stooped to sweep her off her feet. In that brief unguarded moment the hand that held the padlock rose and crashed down on his head, all her deadly fear behind the blow, and her assailant slid unconscious to the floor.

Only then, as she drew a deep shuddering breath and stepped over the prostrate body bent on seizing her chance of escape, did she realise that there were two spectators of the ugly scene. Harry, bearing a platter of food, had just ascended the ladder in time to see the final phase of the struggle. Will, a bucket of water in one hand, was half way up, his head and shoulders protruding through the trap, eyes and mouth wide in astonishment and not a little admiration. "Good for the little 'un," trembled on his lips, but discretion revived and he waited for Harry to speak. The girl faced them, crouched like a tiger-cat ready to spring, the padlock clutched in a determined hand.

"Now just you put that there padlock down, Missy," said Harry severely. "I don't want to hurt you and I'm not even saying you wasn't right to do what you done. But if it comes to a fight betwixt you and me, you'll find my knife's a sight quicker than yon lump of iron." And he pulled out the evil glittering thing and flourished it with impressive effect. Clemency hesitated. She knew she could not hope to outmatch two vigorous and watchful men, but she was loth to surrender the instrument of her salvation.

Harry saw the hesitation and pressed his advantage. "Be sensible, Miss. Neither me nor Will'll do you a mite of harm. And as for Dan'l there — well you've cooled his blood for him. Don't know as I've seen anything neater in all my puff, and serve him right, says I. Never could let a lass alone. But we'll not let him next nor nigh you again. You're worth a lot o' money to us so long as you're safe and well, so stands to reason we'll take good care of you. See, I'd brought you a bite of supper, and Will there has brought you some water. We 'adn't got no milk. But there's a sup o' gin if you've a fancy for that," he added with unwonted generosity, inspired by his private satisfaction in seeing Dan get his comeuppance for once.

In its peculiar warped way it was an honest approach. An appeal for freedom would be useless. She was 'worth a lot of money'. But within his limits he would treat her decently.

"Very well," she said, and came a step or two towards him, the padlock extended on her open palm. He took it from her and dropped it into a capacious pocket. "That's more like it," he said, not unkindly, and the knife disappeared to join the padlock.

"Now here's your victuals, Miss, and Will, set the bucket here against the wall. I can't leave you the lantern, case you set the place afire, so you'll have to manage as best you can by moonlight." He jerked his head towards one end of the loft where a number of small round holes pierced the stone, allowing a faint light to filter in. "There's plenty of hay, so you'll be snug enough. Will — bring up one of those horse blankets for the lady."

Will departed. Harry went on seriously, "But don't be thinking you can get away, just because you're not tied up. This ladder goes down into the stallion's loose box — and he's a killer. You'd be mashed to bloody pulp inside of two minutes if you tried it."

With a vivid memory of the great black brute that had come at them from the hedge, the vicious head, the laid back ears, and the wicked bloodshot eyes, Clemency did not doubt it. Her heart sank, but she maintained a steady composure and thanked Harry politely for both the food and the warning. Will came back with the blanket and then helped Harry to lower the still senseless Pelly down the ladder.

It was while they were so engaged that Clemency at last identified the lad as Will Overing. When last she had seen him his hair had been neatly cropped. Now it had grown long and hung in wild elf locks about his narrow gypsy face. But when he shook it back in order to watch his footing on the ladder, she knew him at once. Some instinctive caution prevented her from proclaiming this discovery, yet somehow, in spite of his obvious association with the highwaymen, it lit a tiny spark of hope. Will was a part of her safe familiar world. He could not, she felt, be wholly evil. There might be some way in which she could appeal to him or bribe him to help her — but not in front of Harry.

With this small gleam of comfort to support her spirits she ate the food that had been brought her and drank some of the water from her cupped hands. She must do all she could to keep up her strength so as to be ready to snatch at any chance of escape. With this brave resolve she made her preparations for sleep, feeling about her in the darkness until she found her cloak and then scooping herself a nest in the hay. Her movements disturbed the stallion in the stable below, and he uttered a shrill squeal of protest. She shuddered. Then she curled herself into the refuge she had made, pulled the blanket over her and composed herself resolutely to get what sleep she could.

In the cottage, the groaning cursing Pelly, having come to his senses upon having a bucket of cold water thrown over him, was clutching his aching head and listening morosely to Harry's eloquence on the subject of tampering with a girl who represented a fortune for both of them. "Why, you might have done for her! Them plucky little ones, they never gives in. They fights you till they dies. And what would Barney have had to say about *that*? So *I'm* speaking *my* mind for once. I'm not letting you near that wench again. Stable key's in my keeping, and there it stops."

In his present state of physical misery Pelly had temporarily lost interest in all females. He grunted surly submission, but added a rider to the effect that if the ransom was not forthcoming he should have his pleasure of the girl without interference or rivalry. Harry agreed to that quite amiably — it was a matter of indifference to him. He was more concerned with the means to be used in collecting the money and in ensuring their own safety while engaged in that ticklish task.

"Reckon I've got that worked out," said Pelly. "We'll have it left at the foot of the gallows post at Buckstone cross roads at midnight next Saturday. That'll take care that there's no one about, for no one in his senses would linger in such a spot at that hour unless he had business there."

Harry signified approval.

"Full of the moon on Sunday, so we shall be able to spot any sign of trickery," continued Pelly, ticking off each cogent point on his fingers. "Also, with four roads meeting, who's to say which one we'll use, either coming or going?"

"It would need a company of militia to stop the place properly," agreed Harry with satisfaction.

"They'll not call in troops," said Pelly confidently. "We'd be bound to see them on the move, and then it would be all up with Missy, as well they do know."

Harry chewed over the details carefully in his slower moving mind. Then he said, "And who's to tell them all this?"

"Missy shall write a letter," said Pelly. "I'm a moderate penman myself, but her hand of write'll carry more conviction. And you'd best warn her not to put in aught but what you tell her — for I can read as well as the next one."

Harry could see no fault with this plan save their lack of writing materials, and Will could easily purchase those, along with the fresh supplies of food which they would now need. And since that seemed to cover all their requirements for the immediate future, they settled down to finish the gin.

Chapter Seventeen

THE Limp and rather grubby missive — it had suffered from sharing Will's pocket with a half eaten apple — was delivered at Ash Croft just before noon on Wednesday. Her parents still lingering in York, for since they could do nothing to help it had been decided that they should not be apprised of the new tragedy that had befallen the unfortunate family, it fell to Prudence, on seeing that familiar script, to open the letter. She perused its contents with a fast beating heart, and after a second, more careful, reading, set out at once to carry it to the Manor. At least it assured her that her sister was alive, and though paper and ink were of the cheapest and the pen had sadly needed mending, the writing itself was clear and firm. The matter had obviously been dictated by Clee's captors and simply described the way in which the ransom was to be paid over. It ended by saying that she was well treated, and begged her friends not to try to trace her, since at the first sign of any such attempt her jailers would disappear, and in that case there was no knowing what her fate would be.

Finding the Manor deserted by all but the servants, Prudence waited with what patience she might, reading and re-reading the letter, though indeed by now she had it by heart, and taking what comfort she could from the strength and steadiness of the writing and the fact that it was undoubtedly Clemency's own. Being fortunately unacquainted with villainy, the threat implicit in the last paragraph missed its mark.

Piers was the first to arrive, and that merely for a change of horses, the grey, Sultan, that he had ridden since dawn being completely done up. Piers looked pretty done up himself, thought Prudence compassionately. Since Clemency's abduction he had spent long hours in the saddle ranging the countryside, only surrendering to the need for sleep during the brief period of complete darkness after moonset. He had lost weight, so that the high cheekbones showed stark beneath the bronzed skin, and the resolute jaw angled more grimly than ever.

When Prudence mutely held out the letter, the light that glowed for a moment in his eyes was betrayal enough, even if she had not already guessed his feelings for her twin.

As she had done herself, he read it first greedily, then more slowly, as though savouring the strength of every stroke and curve traced by those small beloved fingers. A little of the weariness disappeared from his bearing, and he actually sat down for a few minutes, long booted legs stretched out in unaccustomed ease. "At least we know she's alive," he said with deep, prayerful thankfulness. For a moment he brooded on the ineffable relief of this thought. Then he was on his feet again, striding about the floor, his tired brain seeking to wring every scrap of information from the letter.

Lady Eleanor and Giles came in some ten minutes later, just as he was on the point of departure. He lingered to hear their comments on the letter, and their report. For a third time the spluttering lines were devoured and digested by anxious eyes. The newcomers were at one in avering their confidence in the writer's health, insisting that any vagaries were due to the shocking pen that had been used, protesting perhaps a little too much in their eagerness to give comfort, until Pru said, "Yes — perhaps — but she must have been sadly distraught, for it is not like Clee to make so lavish and peculiar a use of capital letters."

Without apology Piers put out a hand and twitched the letter from his aunt's grasp. "I had not noticed," he said shortly, "being unacquainted with Miss Longden's usual style. Yes. I see. There we have 'brought Over to the cross roads', and 'left In plain sight', and 'beg you Will not try to trace me'. Could there be a hidden message in those words?"

But Giles was already exclaiming in excitement, and Lady Eleanor had sprung to her feet, face alight with eagerness.

"Will Overing," they exclaimed, almost in unison. And Giles added, "It fits, Mama! It fits!"

Between them, with many interruptions and corrections, they poured out their story. That morning they had stayed for a nuncheon at the inn at Follifoot, and over the simple meal had pursued their usual tactics of enquiring casually as to the state of trade and the incidence of strangers, drawing, as usual, a complete blank. But when Giles had gone to settle the reckoning the landlady had shyly asked if he would be so kind as to bear a message to her cousin. She was, she explained, cousin to Mrs. Grant, his gardener's wife, and she thought that the Grants would be pleased to have good news of their nephew, Will. She had seen quite a bit of Will over the past week or so. He had been coming in regularly, buying supplies for his employers. He had found a job, she explained, with some horse dealers. He might do well, the way he had with horses.

Giles had shown a proper interest in Overing's welfare, and the good woman had become quite loquacious, even saying, with a demure look, that she believed the lad was courting. The Grants would be pleased to hear *that*, she knew, since they had always disapproved the close attachment between Will and their daughter Elspeth, who were first cousins any way, apart from Will's harum-scarum ways. When Lady Eleanor had enquired the name of Will's new inamorata, the landlady had admitted that she did not know. But he had asked her to get him a comb and some hair ribbons, and then, of all things, he had borrowed paper and ink and a pen. That could only mean love letters and courtship.

To Lady Eleanor and her son, driving back to the Manor as fast as Chevalier could take them, it suggested something quite different. It had brought back to Giles's memory the brief impression of that third figure, dimly seen, who had leapt to Chevalier's head on that fatal night. He would not care to swear to it, but that figure could well have been young Overing's, the comb and ribbons bought for a captive, not a sweetheart. They agreed that the tale hung together quite credibly, and with the confirmation supplied by Clemency's letter they were convinced that the search had narrowed to the vicinity of Follifoot.

Piers had already spread out the map and marked the place with a heavy black line. Now he suddenly said, "Nab Hill! A scant four miles away. I wonder if our highwayman is the same enterprising fellow who tried to stop *me*? What's more it's not so far from the Buckstone crossroads."

"Then Clemency might even be held in that horrid cottage," contributed Lady Eleanor with a shudder. "Or have you already searched that area, Piers?"

"No. And since there seems at least a fair chance that it is the place we want, we must move with great care." He stood in deep thought for several minutes and then nodded decisively. "This is the way we'll do it. We'll drive down the Otley road past the end of the farm lane, and in a hired chaise, too, so that there is no risk of recognition. For if Overing *is* one of the band he would soon spot any of our turnouts and make a pretty good guess as to the occupants and their errand. We can tell at a glance if the lane has been used recently. If it has, then we embark on a closer search when the moon is up."

"Could I come too?" asked Prudence. "If you are only going to drive past the place, I should be no hindrance. It is dreadful just sitting at home waiting for news."

Piers smiled at her sympathetically. "Indeed you may come, and Aunt Eleanor too, if she wishes. In fact a chaise carrying two ladies with their escorts would be less noticeable than one in which two gentlemen travel alone."

There was still more than an hour of precious daylight left by the time that they were ready for the road. No one seemed much inclined for conversation. Too much rested on the outcome of their mission. Once Piers showed the ladies how easy it was to detect freshly made tracks in the heavy hoar frost that crusted the turf where the sun had failed to penetrate, but the journey passed mostly in silence until they were approaching Nab Hill.

"Over the next crest," said Piers. "You'll see the place on the left. It stands well back from the road, but you can see it quite plainly through the trees now that the leaves are down."

The postilions had been instructed at the outset to maintain a brisk but steady pace, neither dawdling along so as to attract suspicion nor springing the horses in such a way as to make close observation difficult. The four passengers sat more erect, taut with expectation and eager eyed for the signs that Piers had indicated. Now they were trotting past the dilapidated gate that gave access to the overgrown lane. Pru held her breath. Giles gave a muted whoop of triumph. Then they were past, and the horses were being checked for the steep descent, while three excited voices, all speaking together, poured out the particular details that they had noted. Only Piers was silent, keen eyes still scanning the building and their setting. Then the road plunged between high stone walls, and the lonely cottage was lost to sight.

"There was no smoke from the chimney," cried Lady Eleanor. "I looked especially for that."

"They'd not risk it during daylight," explained Giles. "You can see smoke for miles. Someone would be sure to come and investigate."

"It must be dreadfully cold," his mother said, with a sympathetic shiver. "Poor Clemency. If she really *is* there," she ended in sudden doubt.

"Well *someone* is certainly using the place," said Piers. "There were signs that the gate has been dragged open recently. It has sagged on its hinges, so the soil was pushed up into a ridge. And there were clear footprints and hoof marks made since the frost set in. Tonight will show whether it is those we seek."

"Do you plan to mount a rescue operation tonight, then?" asked Giles.

"I wish I might think so, but I fear not," said his cousin regretfully. "At present all is conjecture. It may be that travelling tinkers or gypsies are using the place. But even if we find that Miss Longden is indeed held there, we have still to discover just how she is secured and guarded before we dare attempt her rescue. Remember — we shall have only one chance."

The grave warning banished the air of hopeful anticipation which, at the first glimmer of possible success, had sprung up among the little party.

"Then what do you propose?" asked Giles.

"I'll make a reconnaissance tonight. We still have two days of grace left to us. If we could establish that this is the place we are seeking, we shall be in a much stronger position. Even if, in the final outcome, we have to pay the ransom that the scoundrels are asking, we might well effect a rescue while they are picking up their ill-gotten gains."

"But I thought — Giles said — we could not possibly raise such a sum," demurred Prudence.

"No, that is not the difficulty," explained Piers. "Remember that your father's income has been accumulating untouched these four years past. I daresay he could raise double the amount. But since I took it upon myself to withhold the demand, the responsibility is mine. I have already arranged for the money to be available if it is needed."

Even his aunt and cousin looked a little startled at this. To be sure he had spoken quite openly of being pretty well to pass, but since he displayed no ostentatious signs of wealth they had never thought to speculate on the size of his fortune. Lady Eleanor said, rather hesitantly, "Then if her Papa is well able too meet such a call on his purse, why do we not just pay? It seems to me that in any attempt at rescue, more lives must be at risk."

"There are several reasons," said Piers slowly, "sound ones, I believe. There is the need to deliver Miss Longden from her miserable and dangerous situation as swiftly as possible. Consider. She — a tenderly nurtured child — has already been kept in conditions of deadly fear and privation for days. What must her state be? Then there is the fact that we cannot trust her captors to keep their word and hand over their hostage unharmed. In addition to this," he went on, smiling a little, tight lipped, "I have an unconscionable objection to enriching criminals, and thereby encouraging them to repeat their villainies elsewhere. You may set it down to my Yorkshire birth and blood. I'll submit to being fleeced if I must. But it will go sorely against the grain."

"And good valid reasons," agreed Giles heartily. "I'm with you, all the way. Is that the sum of it, then?"

There was a brief silence. Then Piers looked up. But though he met his cousin's gaze straitly enough, he did not seem to see him, nor, indeed, to be aware that he was not alone. For once the fury that had been so rigidly suppressed lest it impair his judgement was plainly to be seen. The blue eyes were incandescent with it. "No," he said, quite gently. "There is one more small matter. Once my darling is safe out of their hands, I am anxious to try a fall with these gentry myself. The world, I think, will be a sweeter, cleaner place, when I have rid it of the vermin that dared to use her so."

Chapter Eighteen

IT was just on nine o'clock when Piers completed his preparations. The hour was earlier than he would have chosen, since the inhabitants of the derelict cottage might still be astir, but moonset was at midnight, and some light was essential. He had refused Giles's earnest plea to accompany him. One determined man could discover all that was to be learned. Two would only double the risk of detection. Giles had to be content with a promise that when the time for action came, he should certainly have a part in it. Meanwhile he was surveying his cousin's activities with deep interest.

Piers had begun by demanding flannel boots for his horse. The clink of shoe on stone would carry far on frosty air, and the quarry would be fully alert to such an indication of an alien presence. Heavy woollen stockings borrowed from Beach to pull over his own footgear came next, and he was already wearing dark clothing. But Giles stared open-mouthed when he asked for a pail of soot from the chimney and proceeded to rub this unusual cosmetic into the skin of his hands and face and throat. He smiled at Giles's expression, white teeth gleaming oddly in his blackened visage, and said that he had got the idea from watching the black fellows in Australia, who could literally melt away into the bush. "Quite often, in poor light, the best way of taking cover is to keep perfectly still," he explained, and advised them not to wait up for him as there was no telling how long his explorations would take.

They watched horse and rider disappear down the avenue. "Though I couldn't possibly sleep, and don't mean to go to bed until he is safe home again," said Lady Eleanor. The hours of waiting stretched endlessly ahead. One could not concentrate on a book, and no one had the heart for playing cards when Giles suggested that way of passing the time. Conversation, too, was desultory, until Giles was called away to look at one of the in-foal mares who was near her time and was giving some cause for anxiety. The two ladies were then able to find some relief by discussing Piers's astonishing outburst in the chaise. At the time no one had said a word, and Piers himself seemed unaware that he had spoken aloud and had gone on, after a brief brooding silence, to discuss such every day topics as the phase of the moon, the weather and which horse he would choose for his projected expedition, quite as though he had said nothing out of the ordinary.

"And what could one have replied?" demanded Lady Eleanor of the interested Prudence. "What *does* one say, when one's nephew betrays in one breath that he has fallen deep in love, and in the next one calmly announces his intention of committing murder as though it was the most natural thing in the world. One can scarcely just wish him happy! *Or* express the hope that his plans will prosper! Though I must confess that I feel for him wholeheartedly on both counts."

The gentleman in question was at that moment happier than had been for some days, and so far his plans were indeed prospering. He had gained entrance without difficulty to an empty hen house which stood scarce a quarter of a mile from his goal and which provided both shelter and concealment for his horse. He was now slipping shadow-like in the shelter of the wall towards the back of the cottage. To be on the move, with some hope at last of bringing help and comfort to his little love, relieved in part the hideous imaginings to which he had been a prey since her disappearance.

He had reached the corner of the wall and paused to listen. Close at hand was an outbuilding — stable or barn — and beyond it, across a yard, the cottage itself, dark and silent. Swiftly he crossed the open space that separated him from the outbuilding, and in that minute heard a horse whicker and the shrill answering squeal of a stallion. So *there* were horses stabled here. And Giles had spoken of a stallion.

The yard lay in full moonlight. Crossing it, he would be clearly visible to any watcher. It was also littered with broken and discarded implements. He made out a rusted plough and two ancient cart wheels, a yoke and a battered bucket, and as he stood mentally charting these treacherous obstacles his ears were assailed by a scraping creaking noise coming from the direction of the house. He slid back into the shadow of the barn. The noise came again, ending, this time, with the crunch of a door pushed firmly home. Someone had come out of the house and footsteps were approaching the stable. He heard the clank of a bucket set down, and then the groan of a rusty lock yielding unwillingly to the key.

Sheer chance had favoured him. Never before had Will visited the stable so late at night. But that very morning Rufus had slipped on a patch of ice and come down, straining a fetlock, and Pelly had permitted Will to poultice the injury afresh before settling down for the night.

To speak the truth, Will preferred the stable to the cottage, and wished he might sleep in the straw with the horses, but those two 'ud never let him. They didn't like him out of their sight for long, and they didn't like him talking to the girl. They had taken to locking him into his room at night, fearful that he might decide to change sides. He only wished he dared. But Pelly's tales of the gang's ways with traitors had scared him to the marrow, and against his terror, pity for the captive paled to insignificance. If he remembered uneasily how Elspeth had spoken of Miss Clemency's kindness and how she had helped her trim a bonnet to wear to church, he salved his discomfort by buying her a comb and some ribbons for her hair. Her hairpins had been lost among the hay in her struggle with Pelly. She had braided her hair to keep it from getting hopelessly tangled, and had tied the braids with wisps of hay until Will had brought her the ribbons.

Now, as he locked the door behind him and went to Rufus's stall, he called up to reassure her. "It's only me, Miss. Will. I'm putting a fresh poultice on Rufus."

The listener outside did not hear what the girl answered, perhaps because of the ecstatic leap of his own heart. Such luck was almost unbelievable. In a rush of exultation he felt that Fate had at last chosen to smile on him, so much so that he was sorely tempted to make his rescue bid at once. It was only a matter of lying hid until Overing came out of the stable, knocking him out, and taking the key. But his own warning sounded in his ears. "Only the one chance." Without further investigation it was too dangerous. They might, for instance, have chained her. The very thought made him grind his teeth in impotent rage — but did not alter the fact that he had no tool for cutting chains. Better to stick to the original and sensible plan, try to establish communication, and work out a scheme that would cover all eventualities.

It was some time before Will finally re-locked the stable and went back to the cottage. While he waited, Piers made a careful survey of the outside of the building. Apart from the big door which Will had used, the only other means of access was a square opening high up in one gable end, which had been used aforetime for lifting hay straight from the wain into the loft. Its wooden cover was probably bolted into position, but without a ladder it was impossible to establish which way it opened. In the other gable was a series of small round holes. Piers judged that pigeons had probably been kept here. It might be possible, if he could reach the roof, to speak to the prisoner through one of those holes.

When Will had gone, he waited patiently for a considerable time, until he felt that the inhabitants of the cottage would surely have settled for the night, and then made his way to the back of the barn where the yard wall joined it. Climbing the wall was child's play, but heaving himself up on to the roof was more tricky. The thatch was rotten, and it would not do to leave a hole in it to advertise his nocturnal visit. He managed at last to find a spot where the thatch had already fallen away to expose solid timber which enabled him to pull himself up, and then wriggled his way cautiously to the end nearest the cottage where the pigeon entries were. He moved as carefully as he could, not so much for fear of the risk to his neck on the frost rimed thatch as for the danger of leaving discernible traces. Best to pray for a sudden thaw, he thought grimly, or trust that the tracks would be ascribed to a marauding fox.

As he had estimated, it was just possible, by hanging perilously over the edge of the roof, to put his mouth to one of the orifices in the wall. Another scrap of aboriginal bush lore came to his mind. With lips pressed close to the opening and one hand funnelling the sound while the other anchored him to the roof, he called "Coo-ee," as loudly as he dared. No response. But at least no rough male voice had made sharp outcry, so there was no guard within the stable. He tried again, twice in close succession, and then, tentatively, "Clem-en-cy!" Listening intently he just caught the faint incredulous reply.

"Where are you? Oh please! Where are you?"

"On the roof. Can you move closer to the pigeon entries?" he said slowly and clearly.

There was a pause. He could hear a faint scuffling sound, and then her voice, so close and clear that he hastily bade her hush before she got beyond, "Piers! It *is* you, isn't it?"

"Speak softly," he cautioned. "We're not far from the cottage, and I can hear you very clearly now that you have moved close to the wall. How are you secured and guarded?"

"I'm not tied up any more. I was at first but the only way down is through the loose box, and they leave the stallion there. He's a killer. Harry told me so, and Will says it's true."

"Can you see a small wooden door at the other end of the loft?"

"Yes. I found it the first day, but it won't open from inside."

"Good. Means it *will* open from outside. Listen, love. I daren't stay long. I'll be back tomorrow night with more help and a ladder. We'll have you out of this. Meanwhile, can you play a part? Not betray that I've been in touch with you? Behave just as you have been doing?"

Incredibly there came the sound of a soft chuckle. Not knowing how her spirits were soaring at the very thought of his nearness, so that in spite of cold, dirt and discomfort she was for the moment gloriously happy, he could scarcely believe that his ears had not deceived him. Her voice was confident — amused. "Of course I can. All females can play-act. Anyway, no one but Will comes near me. I think the other two are afraid of me since I hit one of them on the head with a padlock."

Not a hint in that gay young voice of the terror and revulsion that still swept over her at the thought of one man's cruel eyes and greedy mouth. Certainly *one* small female could play-act.

"There are just the three of them?"

"I have seen only three, and Will has not spoken of any others, but I cannot vouch for it."

"And you are well fed and cared for?"

"Well fed enough. Will has been good to me. But oh! So dirty and unkempt and lonely! You cannot think how blissful it is to hear a friend's voice! If only I could see you, and touch you. When you are gone I shall wonder if you were real."

"Real enough, my girl, as I'll willingly prove to you once I have you out of this. You may expect the rescue party tomorrow. Till then, look as despondent as you can. And to help you in such dissimulation you may pass the time in considering the married state, as it is lived in the far Antipodes. *That* should give you a sufficiently anxious and dejected air!"

There was a brief stunned pause. Then an indignant voice, forgetting all about the need for lowering its note, exclaimed, "Piers Kennedy! Are you by any chance proposing marriage? Under *these* circumstances?"

"I am indeed, my darling. Let me assure you that there is a beautiful moon, even if you can't see it. And if a man is so far gone in love — or idiocy — that he proposes marriage through a pigeon entry, while hanging upside down on a damned slippery gable end, at least his beloved may well be convinced of his sincerity, if not of the stability of his wits!"

A tiny silence, while the lady assimilated this. Then a gurgle of laughter. "You pay a pretty compliment, Sir — proposing marriage in one breath and claiming in the next that your wits are disordered! I regret that I am quite untaught in dealing with such pleasantries. Moreover, if you could but see the — object — that you have just honoured, I fear you might withdraw your very obliging offer. The amenities of my prison do not include soap and water!"

"As to that, my sweet, you should see me! Othello in person, though less magnificently dressed. Perhaps you are in the right of it, and we should defer our love making to a more gracious occasion. But I give you fair warning. Your answer had best be favourable, or I may be tempted to try a little abduction on my own account."

There was an impish chuckle, and a mischievous voice said, "In that case, Sir, the answer is certainly, "No". I have always had a yearning for romance in the high old fashioned style."

"Why! You wicked little thing! Count yourself safe behind your impregnable walls, do you, offering such blatant provocation! Just wait till tomorrow and see how I'll deal with you."

"You terrify me, Sir," came back to him, mock meek. "Perhaps after all I had better strive to bring myself to a submissive frame of mind."

"That's a good girl," he said contentedly. "No need to tell *you* to keep a brave heart. Be patient just a little longer — and I'll have Aunt Eleanor buy you the largest cake of soap to be found in Yorkshire! Till tomorrow!"

He held his impatient mount to a walk until they were a good half-mile from the cottage, and then dismounted and removed the flannel boots, an attention welcomed with a snort of approval. He grinned and patted the sheeny neck as he swung up into the saddle again. "And a fine handsome pair we are, to go a-courting," he confided to an attentively flickering ear. "Get on with you, now, and not a word, mind, as to where you've been tonight." He chuckled at his own absurdity as he shook the mare into a trot. They were almost home when suddenly he lifted his head. The mare, obeying the check on the rein, stopped, and her rider sat motionless, his face tilted to the skies.

A man who has served the sea for most of his life is always aware, without conscious thought, of any change in the wind. There was no mistaking it. There was a softening in the air, a dampness that presaged fog and rain. The wind had backed westerly. Piers was not particularly well versed in the outward forms of religious observance. Perhaps the heartfelt, "Thank God!" which the smell of that breeze evoked from his lips was as sincere as any prayer couched in more elegant phrases. His last lingering anxiety was allayed. By morning there would be no traces left to mark his recent activities.

Chapter Nineteen

HE spared a wry grin for the travesty of the classic elopement in which he was destined to play a leading part. The ladder that he and Beach were constructing should, of course, have been of rope; the element of danger supplied by an irate Papa. He had even rejected the time-hallowed owl's hoot as the agreed signal between the rescuers — there were likely to be too many genuine owls in the vicinity. Despite a strong case made out by Beach for the opening bars of Hearts of Oak, they had finally agreed on the first few notes of the British Grenadiers. The military tune was readily recognisable and easy to whistle.

So the ladder was, in fact constructed of wood, in three sections convenient for stowing in the carriage but easily assembled, and so that the enterprise proved successful he would thankfully flout tradition.

The plan for a rescue was simple enough. Beach was to form the outer guard, returning to wait with the carriage as soon as he had helped transport the ladder to the purlieus of the Wyke barn. Giles would be posted at the boundary wall, to give warning of any sign of activity in cottage or lane. Piers himself was to effect the rescue, with a minimum of noise, and to this end had equipped himself with every imaginable necessity for dealing with stubborn rusted bolts.

Lady Eleanor and Prudence had been dispatched to Ilkley, with instructions to buy not only the 'largest cake of soap in Yorkshire' but such other sweet scented unguents and essences as might appeal to the feminine fancy. Also, in a private conversation between aunt and nephew when Pru had run out to speak with Giles, the prettiest bedgown and wrapper that the Ilkley shops could produce.

"Piers!" his aunt had exclaimed, much shocked by such an improper commission. The blue eyes had gleamed wicked mischief at her, but then he had sobered and said quietly, "My poor infant has spent days in wretched squalor. When I bring her back to you tonight, I want her to have every frivolous luxury that we can contrive."

Lady Eleanor's air of severity vanished, despite the wicked look in her nephew's eye as he went on, "I know, dearest, that I shall not be privileged to behold the charming fripperies that you will purchase in my behalf — at least not *yet* — but the future promises well, and, if I have my way, will soon become the present."

"And so you have really lost your heart at last?" she probed gently.

His whole expression softened. "It is all so different," he tried to explain. "Until — well, no matter for that. The thing is that I have always found my work adventure and excitement enough. It *is* exciting, you know, Aunt Eleanor, to make a new, young country yield fruit. I never looked for anything more. But Clemency —" He stopped. Then the blue eyes lifted to hers. "I cannot do without her. I *need* her. And I think she feels the same about me," he said simply.

She could not resist a mild teasing. "I thought that you considered your exciting new country an unsuitable domicile for a delicately bred female," she reminded him.

He had the grace to look abashed, the grave face flushed, as he defended himself in the age old way of lovers. "I did not then know Clemency — her courage, her steadfastness. She will put her hand in mine and come adventuring with me and never a backward glance. And it will be my proud privilege so to cherish her that she shall never regret putting her happiness into my hands."

Pru had come running back then, and the shopping party had set out in good heart, returning considerably later than expected with a quantity of parcels intriguingly wrapped that Mattie was bidden to carry to Miss Clemency's room.

Then it was time to be moving. "No soot tonight?" asked Giles gaily, and expressed deep disappointment when his cousin pronounced it unnecessary.

"We know exactly where we are going and what we have to do. No need to venture into places where we might be picked out by our white skins."

"Pistols, then?" Giles was determined to have his full measure of excitement. And this time Piers nodded.

"A good notion. Though you'll have difficulty with that shoulder of yours. Any use with your left hand?"

Giles shook his head ruefully and unlocked the cabinet which held the late Sir John's small arms. They looked admiringly at his duelling pistols, beautiful and deadly, but by far too long in the barrel for their present purpose. Eventually Giles selected a neat little pocket pistol by Henry Nock while Piers chose a tiny weapon no more than six inches long which

Giles rather thought his father had brought back from Brussels — or was it Liege?

"And remember," cautioned Piers, as his cousin re-locked the cabinet, "no chivalrous notions. These people are probably murderers half a dozen times over, and *they* will have no scruples. If we are attacked, shoot, and shoot to kill. Clemency's life as well as your own may depend upon it."

Giles looked dubious. "I might be able to regard the two big fellows as the vermin they undoubtedly are, but I don't think I could bring myself to shoot Overing," he confessed.

"Indeed no! My apologies, cousin. I was not thinking of him, though if need be you may knock him out with my very good will. But he has been kind to my girl, so he certainly deserves *some* consideration from us."

His conscience relieved on this head, Giles announced his perfect willingness to shoot any number of villainous strangers, whereupon his cousin dryly pointed out that, since there would scarcely be time to reload, he had best make sure of his aim at the first one.

Conditions tonight were so much in contrast to those of his previous sortie that Piers might well be forgiven for feeling that they were Fortune's favourites. A light mizzle of moisture was in the air — half mist, half falling rain — perfectly designed to blanket such small sounds as they might make, and to persuade any sensible comfort-loving highwayman to remain snugly indoors.

In silence and with well practised smoothness the sections of the ladder were carried to the barn and assembled. Beach and Giles then retired to their respective posts while Piers mounted the ladder to the hay port. And again found luck on his side, for the door was held in place by wooden wedges, swollen by the damp but still easy to remove without undue noise. Once he had forced out two or three of them the rest came easily enough, and he was able to pivot the door through the opening and prop it against the wall. And there was Clemency, eager and expectant, and no wall between.

Danger, good sense and the need for haste all forgotten, Piers held wide his arms and Clemency melted into them. For a moment they clung together, her head nestling against his breast, his cheek on her hair. Then he put her from him, urgent fingers still gripping her shoulders.

"Yes?" he whispered.

"Yes, please," she whispered shyly back.

For a moment it seemed that he must snatch her to his heart again, but this time practical considerations prevailed.

"Come then," he said softly. "I'll go first, and you follow close. That way I can steady you if you're nervous."

She managed the awkward business of lowering herself from the floor of the loft to the ladder, his hand ready to guide her feet to the first step. "Just take it easily," said the calm voice. "No need for haste, and I'm here to catch you if you slip." But she accomplished the descent without difficulty, even in the darkness. It seemed that they would be able to effect their withdrawal undetected and without risk of pursuit — and it was in that moment that disaster struck.

The loft door which Piers had left propped against the wall fell over with a resounding thump. Startled, Clemency sprang aside, stumbled against the ladder and brought that down too, and immediately the furious squeal of the stallion blared out into the night.

No one was going to sleep through that racket. Piers swept the girl into his arms and raced for the corner where Giles was peering anxiously towards the cottage. It showed no signs of life as yet, but someone *must* have heard the uproar.

"Get back to Beach as fast as you can," snapped Piers. "Tell him to drive like hell. I'll stand them off to give him a start." He thrust the reluctant girl towards Giles who obediently seized her hand and began to run, pulling her along with him despite her breathless protests.

"Don't be a stubborn little idiot," he shot back at her. "The sooner you're safe away the quicker I can get back to help him."

That made sense. She stopped struggling to pull her hand free and ran as fast as she could, slipping and stumbling on the rough turf, and listening anxiously for any sound of activity from the cottage.

Piers meanwhile had replaced the ladder, climbed it, and pulled it up after him. Fumbling frantically in the darkness he had fitted the fallen door into its framework and propped it into place with the ladder. From the outside a cursory glance would see nothing amiss. Then he felt his way along the wall to the far end of the loft, the space above the loose box, and waited, pistol in hand. It had seemed to him certain that the kidnappers would first visit the loft to discover the cause of the disturbance before commencing a search of the fields, but he could not wholly suppress the horrid thought that they might have heard the departure of the fugitives and started at once in pursuit. So the minutes of waiting lengthened into an agony of doubt as his fears grew that he had miscalculated and had left Clemency and Giles to fall an easy prey to the hunters.

It was with deep thankfulness that he heard at last the sound for which he had been waiting — the scraping of the barn door being pushed open — and saw a square of faint yellow light which indicated the position of the trap door, with the top of the ladder protruding through it. There had indeed been quite a long delay. Pelly had wakened at the stallion's outcry, but had then had to pull on his boots and light the lantern, after which it took some time to rouse Harry from a gin sodden slumber and wrest the key from him. He did not really expect to find anything wrong. Lucifer was still kicking up the deuce of a rumpus, and he had not Overing's knack of quietening the enraged brute. It took time to secure him so that it was safe to mount the ladder. By that time Harry, too, had arrived, blear eyed and cursing, but determined to see that Pelly did not harm the girl who represented a fortune.

Just the two of them. And only one at a time could mount the ladder. Piers thrust the pistol back into his pocket. Best not to fire. The sound of a shot would certainly bring Overing on to the scene, possibly others, and there was no sense in lengthening the odds. He waited, tensed to spring, as the first man stepped through the opening, holding up the lantern to make sure that the prisoner was still there and ripping out a furious oath when he saw that she was not. In that moment, as he swung round to scan the rest of the place, Piers sprang, landing on his shoulders and bringing him to the ground. The lantern fell, shattering the glass and putting out the light. It rolled slowly towards the trap door, hesitated for a moment on the lip, and then, as of deliberate design, gently toppled over, to crash down on the head of the ascending Harry and roll him off the ladder in a flurry of arms and legs, his afflicted head striking the flagstones below with a force that stretched him quiescent on the floor.

Above his unconscious head a desperate battle was fought out in the darkness. It was well for Piers that he had seen a good deal of the seamier side of life and knew in some degree what he might expect. for Pelly was both vigorous and powerful, knew every vicious twist and crippling blow that ever defiled a clean sport, and was capable of swinging the lighter built man clean off his feet by sheer superiority of weight. The initial advantage was with Piers, who, in his surprise attack had succeeded in establishing a half nelson grip on his opponent and was grimly striving to complete the hold that would give him the mastery, while Pelly was straining every sinew to dislodge the incubus that clung so threateningly. Now he kicked up and back, aiming for the groin, but failing to land the disabling blow that he had intended flung himself backward, bearing Piers to the ground pinned beneath the weight of his body. His lips writhed back in a snarl of triumph. But in that instant there came a sharp explosion, and sudden agony wrenched a deep groan from him as his hands clutched wildly at his belly. His tortured convulsions carried him clear of Piers, who, winded by the fall, was sucking air into aching lungs and staggering groggily to his feet, fingers fumbling dazedly for the pocket that had held the pistol. The scorched cloth crumbled, at his touch. The bullet had seared his thigh as the gun exploded, and penetrated his opponent's body, inflicting a wound that was plainly serious, since it had so abruptly terminated the fight.

With the quite illogical intention of seeking aid for the wounded man whom he had done his utmost to kill, Piers began to grope his way towards the ladder, and had just found the trap opening when he heard a familiar air whistled from below.

"You there, Giles? You've made good speed, Kindle a light will you? It's black as the pit up here, and I've wounded one fellow — or rather not I, but your father's pistol." And in reply to Giles's exclamation, "It went off when he threw me, and shot him." Then, urgently, "Did they get clear away?"

Giles reassured him on this head, saying nothing of the dire threats by which it had been achieved. "I promised we'd be close behind them," he was beginning, as the tinder caught alight. "Good God — there's another one!" as the tiny flame revealed the still unconscious Harry. Then his eye fell on the broken lantern with its fragment of candle, and he picked it up and lit it. "That's the fellow that kept guard over me," he recognised. "Best tie him up before he comes to his senses. Must have fallen off the ladder. Drunk, I should think," he added, catching the fumes of gin as he stooped to the task.

"Now — what next?" he enquired, buckling the last strap round Harry's legs. "Had we not best take a look at the house? There may be more of them. And where's young Overing got to?"

This was not long left in doubt. As they stepped into the entry a heavy pounding assailed their ears, and led them to a locked door whence a terrified voice was loudly appealing for aid. Turning the key, they came face to face with the wretched Overing who had wakened at the sound of the shot to the realisation that he was trapped. He cowered away in terror at the sight of his visitors, but with some pains was eventually persuaded into submissive coherence. Then the whole story came tumbling out. Once started, it seemed he could not stop talking, rambling, dramatic, inconsequent, as he hurried about helping Piers carry the wounded man from the loft and bestow the hapless Harry in the cottage kitchen.

Pelly had sunk into a semi-stupor, muttering and groaning from time to time, but obviously unaware of his surroundings. By the look of him it seemed improbable that he would survive to face the hangman. Discussion between the two cousins as to which of them should remain at the cottage and which should summon the doctor and the forces of the law, in the person of Constable Trudgeon, to deal with the untidy remnants of the business, reduced Will to a pallid silence once more. Piers addressed him with brusque kindness. "Best be off home, Overing, before we call the constable. I'm told you were good to Miss Longden, so far as you dared, so *I've* no quarrel with you, and my cousin here is uncommon blind when it suits him. See that you choose your masters more wisely in future."

The remark, intended only to terminate an awkward interview on a mildly humorous note, produced an unexpected result. Will dropped clumsily to his knees. "Yes, Sir," he said worshipfully. "I'll serve *you*, Sir, an you'll take me. You'll be able to use me some ways, in those queer outlandish parts where you're a-going, and I swear I'll be faithful and hard working. I've learned my lesson. Try me, Sir."

Giles protested that the youngster had done nothing to show himself worthy of trust, but Piers, in his own relief and thankfulness at the safe outcome of the affair, was in more generous mood. Perhaps he did not put a great deal of faith in Will's protestations, but he nodded acceptance, and with that gesture, had he but known it, bound the lad to him in unfaltering loyalty. In years to come, Will Overing was to display two faded strips of silk ribbon to his grandchildren and weave wondrous tales of how the buying of those ribbons had changed the whole course of his life. But for the moment Piers was too intent on rejoining Clemency and relieving her anxiety to pay more than impatient attention to Will's fervent thanks.

"Off you go then, lad. Your uncle will be pleased to see you home, I know. Now, Giles, if you'll stay here till Trudgeon relieves you of your charges, I'll get back to the Manor as soon as I've informed that honest fellow of the harvest awaiting his collection here," and scarcely waiting on his cousin's assent he was swinging into the saddle — for Giles had brought the horses in while his cousin and Overing dealt with the prisoners — and waving a gay farewell was off at a dangerously headlong pace.

Chapter Twenty

LADY ELEANOR was adamant. The child had taken her bath and was tucked up in bed with a glass of hot milk for sustenance and her sister to bear her company. Yes, of course she would take up a message at once, for both girls were desperately anxious, but she could not possibly permit him to see Clemency tonight. Not his best efforts at cajolery could soften her determination, and eventually he had to admit defeat and wend his way home, pausing in the stables for a word with Giles who had just come in.

But it was no more than ten next morning when he presented himself at the Manor. For once he had taken particular pains with his appearance, and was wearing a beautifully cut coat of dark green superfine with the dove-grey pantaloons that made him look taller than ever. Having endured some ribald comment on this unusual magnificence from his affectionate cousin, he was allowed to ascend to the breakfast room where his aunt and Pru were dawdling over the coffee cups, in what Aunt Eleanor described as disgraceful laziness, after the strain of the past week. Clemency had been ordered to take breakfast in bed, although both ladies admitted that she seemed little the worse for her ordeal, and was, in fact, in tearing spirits.

"I suppose you will wish to see her alone," said Lady Eleanor indulgently. "Well — you may do so in the little parlour at the turn of the stairs. I will send her to you as soon as she is ready."

But when Piers pushed open the parlour door, the room was already occupied. Having appointed this secluded little room as a suitable meeting place for lovers, Lady Eleanor had caused a fire to be kindled there, and kneeling on the hearth was Clemency, combing long silken tresses still damp and rosemary scented from their recent washing. Lady Eleanor had forbidden her to wash her hair the previous evening. "Enough to give you your death," she had declared. "Quite out of the question. Why, it must take hours to dry such a quantity properly."

But this morning, left to her own devices, she had only toyed with the tempting breakfast that Pru had brought her. She was too excited to be hungry, for Piers would be coming soon, she knew. And not for worlds would she have him see her with her hair in this lank and dismal state. She had coaxed Mattie into helping her to comb out the tangles and then to wash it. Now at last she felt cleansed of the contamination of Pelly's touch. It was Mattie who had suggested that after a vigorous towelling she should dry the gleaming mass before the parlour fire.

Absorbed in her rhythmic combing and lost in a private dream, she did not hear the door open and was unaware of Piers's presence until a teasing voice behind her said softly, "Clean enough now for kisses?"

She jumped, and cried out at him for startling her so, but he paid little heed to the pretended scolding, his hands catching hers to lift her to her feet and then sliding up to her shoulders to draw her close.

"A mermaiden weaving her spells," he said softly into the silky curtain that hung about her. "Am I not already fast in your toils? A helpless but very willing prisoner."

That made her laugh and look up at him, as he had intended, and he stooped swiftly to kiss her mouth, gently at first, and then, as he felt her snuggle contentedly into his hold, more possessively.

Clemency had dreamed of those kisses, had clung for comfort in her captivity to that strangely sweet memory of their first encounter. It was no demure simpering miss that he held in his arms, but a warm vital young creature, deeply in love. Her arms went up about his neck and she returned his embrace with a mingled eagerness and shyness that he found enchanting. But presently slim fingers tugged gently at his hair, and he raised his head to look down at her questioningly. There was a tiny pucker on her brow.

"What is it, my sweet?"

She took his hand and held it lovingly against her cheek. "It was just something Lady Eleanor once said — that you had told Giles you meant never to marry — that Australia was no place for a woman. Not that I care for *that*, of course, for there's nothing I would like better than to travel the world with you. But are you quite sure you really want to marry me?"

"Little doubter," he mocked, and made to pull her close again, but she held him off with a quaint air of determination, and he waited for what more she would say.

Her colour had risen and he could see a tiny pulse throbbing in her throat. "I wanted to be sure —" and now her eyes were anywhere but on his face — "that you were not offering for me out of some antiquated notion of chivalry. I mean — I do realise the awkwardness of my situation. No one knows where I have been these past five days. And even if the truth were known my reputation must still be sadly blown upon."

She was perfectly serious. He had not thought it possible to love her more, but the funny mixture of innocence and dignity, the determination not to take advantage of him, made him ache with protective tenderness.

"You rate my notions of chivalry too high, my little love. I'm a hard-bitten ogre — remember? Or had you forgot that I'm not versed in the code of behaviour proper to a gentleman? No, my girl. I'm going to marry you because I can't help myself. And as for Australia not being a fit place for a woman — well — you've given me ample proof that *you're* not safe, even in Yorkshire. In the three months since I've known you I've seen you try to starve yourself to death, so that there's no more than one sweet mouthful left for your ogre to gobble up; you've been kidnapped and held to ransom; and as if that weren't enough to turn a man's hair white" — he shook that silver streaked head at her menacingly — "I cannot help recalling the outrageously improper way in which you approach perfectly strange men! Why! Claiming you in marriage is the only way I can hope to get any peace of mind! I'll have you in safe keeping — mine — where I can deal adequately with your crazy starts. At our very first meeting I was aware that you stood in dire need of a masterful hand. It was only because, on such short acquaintance, I could not spank you, that I kissed you — and see where that has brought us!" and he demonstrated, to her great content.

And then yielding to irresistible temptation, he lifted a strand of the shining hair to his lips, his eyes meeting hers in dancing mischief above it, as he said, "Your hair is very beautiful, my darling. I wish that you might always wear it so — unbound and uncovered — but to the end of my days I shall never cease to cherish the memory of that absurd, adorable bonnet."

*

If you enjoyed *Quality Maid*, please share your thoughts on Amazon by leaving a review.

For more free and discounted eBooks every week, sign up to our newsletter.

Follow us on Twitter, Facebook and Instagram.

Printed in Great Britain
by Amazon

17813341R00082